Memory: How to Develop, Train and Use It

BESTSELLING NON-FICTION

- Gravity by George Gamow
  Sciences/Physics, ISBN: 9789388118705
- How to Develop Self-Confi. and Pub. Speaking by Dale Carnegie
  Mind, Body & Spirit, ISBN: 9789388118286
- How to Stop Worrying and Start Living by Dale Carnegie
  Mind, Body & Spirit, ISBN: 9789387669161
- How to Win Friends and Influence People by Dale Carnegie
  Self Help/General, ISBN: 9789387669178
- Mein Kampf by Adolf Hitler
  Autobiographies/Leaders, ISBN: 9789387669260
- My Experiments with Truth by Mahatma Gandhi
  Autobiographies/Leaders, ISBN: 9789387669277
- Relativity by Albert Einstein
  Sciences/Physics, ISBN: 9789387669185
- The Art of War by Sun Tzu
  Self Help/Success, ISBN: 9789387669321
- The Diary of a Young Girl by Anne Frank
  Autobiographies/Memoirs, ISBN: 9789387669208
- The Magic of Believing by Claudie Bristol
  Religion/Christianity, ISBN: 9789388118217
- The Miracles of Your Mind by Joseph Murphy
  Mind, Body & Spirit, ISBN: 9789387669215
- The Power of Your Subconscious Mind by Joseph Murphy
  Mind, Body & Spirit, ISBN: 9789387669222
- The Richest Man in Babylon by George S. Clason
  Business & Economics, ISBN: 9789388118354
- Think and Grow Rich by Napoleon Hill
  Self Help/Success, ISBN: 9789387669352

Search the book by its ISBN

MEMORY

How to Develop Train and Use It

WILLIAM WALKER ATKINSON

GENERAL PRESS

Published by
GENERAL PRESS
4805/24, Fourth Floor, Krishna House
Ansari Road, Daryaganj, New Delhi - 110002
Ph : 011-23282971, 45795759
E-mail : generalpressindia@gmail.com

www.generalpress.in

First Edition : 2021

ISBN : 9789354990069

Published by Azeem Ahmad Khan for General Press

Contents

1. Memory: Its Importance. 7
2. Cultivation of the Memory. 14
3. Celebrated Cases of Memory 20
4. Memory Systems 26
5. The Subconscious Record-File 33
6. Attention 39
7. Association. 46
8. Phases of Memory 53
9. Training the Eye. 59
10. Training the Ear 66
11. How to Remember Names. 72
12. How to Remember Faces 78
13. How to Remember Places. 84
14. How to Remember Numbers 90

15. How to Remember Music 98

16. How to Remember Occurrences. 103

17. How to Remember Facts 108

18. How to Remember Words, Etc. 114

19. How to Remember Books, Plays, Tales, Etc. 119

20. General Instructions. 126

Chapter 1

Memory: Its Importance

It needs very little argument to convince the average thinking person of the great importance of memory, although even then very few begin to realize just how important is the function of the mind that has to do with the retention of mental impressions. The first thought of the average person when he is asked to consider the importance of memory, is its use in the affairs of every-day life, along developed and cultivated lines, as contrasted with the lesser degrees of its development. In short, one generally thinks of memory in its phase of "a good memory" as contrasted with the opposite phase of "a poor memory." But there is a much broader and fuller meaning of the term than that of even this important phase.

It is true that the success of the individual in his every-day business, profession, trade or other occupation depends very materially upon the possession of a good memory. His value in any walk in life depends to a great extent upon the degree of memory he may have developed. His memory of faces, names, facts, events, circumstances and other things concerning his every-day work is the measure of his ability to accomplish his task. And in the social intercourse of men and women, the possession of a retentive memory, well stocked with available facts, renders its possessor a desirable member of society. And in the higher activities of thought, the memory comes as an invaluable aid to the individual in marshalling the bits and sections of knowledge he may have acquired, and passing them in review before his cognitive faculties—thus does the soul review its mental possessions. As Alexander Smith has said: "A man's real possession is his memory; in nothing else is he rich; in nothing else is the poor." Richter has said: "Memory is the only paradise from which we cannot be driven away. Grant but memory to us, and we can lose nothing by death." Lactantius says: "Memory tempers prosperity, mitigates adversity, controls youth, and delights old age."

But even the above phases of memory represent but a small segment of its complete circle. Memory is more than "a good memory"—it is the means whereby we perform the largest share of our mental work. As Bacon has said: "All knowledge is but remembrance." And Emerson: "Memory is a primary and fundamental faculty, without which none other can work: the cement, the bitumen, the matrix in which the other faculties are embedded. Without it all life and thought were an unrelated succession." And Burke: "There is no faculty of the mind which can bring its energy into effect unless the memory be stored with ideas for it to look upon." And Basile: "Memory is the cabinet of imagination, the treasury of reason, the registry of conscience, and the council chamber of thought." Kant pronounced memory to be "the most wonderful of the faculties." Kay, one of the best authorities on the subject has said, regarding it: "Unless the mind possessed the power of treasuring up and recalling its past experiences, no knowledge of any kind could be acquired. If every sensation, thought, or emotion passed entirely from the mind the moment it ceased to be present, then it would be as if it had not been; and it could not be recognized or named should it happen to return. Such an one would not only be without knowledge,—without experience gathered from the past,—but without purpose, aim, or plan regarding the future, for these imply knowledge and require memory. Even voluntary motion, or motion for a purpose, could have no existence without memory, for memory is involved in every purpose. Not only the learning of the scholar, but the inspiration of the poet, the genius of the painter, the heroism of the warrior, all depend upon memory. Nay, even consciousness itself could have no existence without memory for every act of consciousness involves a change from a past state to a present, and did the past state vanish the moment it was past, there could be no consciousness of change. Memory, therefore, may be said to be involved in all conscious existence—a property of every conscious being!"

In the building of character and individuality, the memory plays an important part, for upon the strength of the impressions received, and the firmness with which they are retained, depends the fibre of character and individuality. Our experiences are indeed the stepping stones to greater attainments, and at the same time our guides and protectors from danger. If the memory serves us well in this respect we are saved the pain of repeating the mistakes of the past, and may also profit by remembering and thus avoiding the mistakes of others. As Beattie says: "When memory is preternaturally defective, experience and knowledge will be deficient in proportion, and imprudent conduct and absurd opinion are the necessary consequence."

Bain says: "A character retaining a feeble hold of bitter experience, or genuine delight, and unable to revive afterwards the impression of the time is in reality the victim of an intellectual weakness under the guise of a moral weakness. To have constantly before us an estimate of the things that affect us, true to the reality, is one precious condition for having our will always stimulated with an accurate reference to our happiness. The thoroughly educated man, in this respect, is he that can carry with him at all times the exact estimate of what he has enjoyed or suffered from every object that has ever affected him, and in case of encounter can present to the enemy as strong a front as if he were under the genuine impression. A full and accurate memory, for pleasure or for pain, is the intellectual basis both of prudence as regards self, and sympathy as regards others."

So, we see that the cultivation of the memory is far more than the cultivation and development of a single mental faculty—it is the cultivation and development of our entire mental being—the development of our *selves*.

To many persons the words memory, recollection, and remembrance, have the same meaning, but there is a great difference in the exact shade of meaning of each term. The student of this book should make the distinction between the terms, for by so doing he will be better able to grasp the various points of advice and instruction herein given. Let us examine these terms.

Locke in his celebrated work, the "Essay Concerning Human Understanding" has clearly stated the difference between the meaning of these several terms. He says: "Memory is the power to revive again in our minds those ideas which after imprinting, have disappeared, or have been laid aside out of sight—when an idea again recurs without the operation of the like object on the external sensory, it is *remembrance*; if it be sought after by the mind, and with pain and endeavor found, and brought again into view, it is *recollection*." Fuller says, commenting on this: "Memory is the power of reproducing in the mind former impressions, or percepts. Remembrance and Recollection are the exercise of that power, the former being involuntary or spontaneous, the latter volitional. We remember because we cannot help it but we recollect only through positive effort. The act of remembering, taken by itself, is involuntary. In other words, when the mind remembers without having tried to remember, it acts spontaneously. Thus it may be said, in the narrow, contrasted senses of the two terms, that we remember by chance, but recollect by intention, and if the endeavor be successful that which is reproduced becomes, by the very effort to bring it forth, more firmly intrenched in the mind than ever."

But the New Psychology makes a little different distinction from that of Locke, as given above. It uses the word memory not only in his sense of "The power to revive, etc.," but also in the sense of the activities of the mind which tend to receive and store away the various impressions of the senses, and the ideas conceived by the mind, to the end that they may be reproduced voluntarily, or involuntarily, thereafter. The distinction between remembrance and recollection, as made by Locke, is adopted as correct by The New Psychology.

It has long been recognized that the memory, in all of its phases, is capable of development, culture, training and guidance through intelligent exercise. Like any other faculty of mind, or physical part, muscle or limb, it may be improved and strengthened. But until recent years, the entire efforts of these memory-developers were directed to the strengthening of that phase of the memory known as "recollection," which, you will remember, Locke defined as an idea or impression "sought after by the mind, and with pain and endeavor found, and brought again into view." The New Psychology goes much further than this. While pointing out the most improved and scientific methods for "re-collecting" the impressions and ideas of the memory, it also instructs the student in the use of the proper methods whereby the memory may be stored with clear and distinct impressions which will, thereafter, flow naturally and involuntarily into the field of consciousness when the mind is thinking upon the associated subject or line of thought; and which may also be "re-collected" by a voluntary effort with far less expenditure of energy than under the old methods and systems.

You will see this idea carried out in detail, as we progress with the various stages of the subject, in this work. You will see that the first thing to do is *to find something to remember*; then to impress that thing clearly and distinctly upon the receptive tablets of the memory; then to exercise the re membrance in the direction of bringing out the stored-away facts of the memory; then to acquire the scientific methods of recollecting special items of memory that may be necessary at some special time. This is the natural method in memory cultivation, as opposed to the artificial systems that you will find mentioned in another chapter. It is not only development of the memory, but also development of the mind itself in several of its regions and phases of activity. It is not merely a method of recollecting, but also a method of correct seeing, thinking and remembering.

This method recognizes the truth of the verse of the poet, Pope, who said: "Remembrance and reflection how allied! What thin partitions sense from thought divide!"

Chapter 2
Cultivation of the Memory

This book is written with the fundamental intention and idea of pointing out a rational and workable method whereby the memory may be developed, trained and cultivated. Many persons seem to be under the impression that memories are bestowed by nature, in a fixed degree or possibilities, and that little more can be done for them—in short, that memories are born, not made. But the fallacy of any such idea is demonstrated by the investigations and experiments of all the leading authorities, as well as by the results obtained by persons who have developed and cultivated their own memories by individual effort without the assistance of an instructor. But all such improvement, to be real, must be along certain natural lines and in accordance with the well established laws of psychology, instead of along artificial lines and in defiance of psychological principles. Cultivation of the memory is a far different thing from "trick memory," or feats of mental legerdemain if the term is permissible.

Kay says: "That the memory is capable of indefinite improvement, there can be no manner of doubt; but with regard to the means by which this improvement is to be effected mankind are still greatly in ignorance." Dr. Noah Porter says: "The natural as opposed to the artificial memory depends on the relations of sense and the relations of thought,—the spontaneous memory of the eye and the ear availing itself of the obvious conjunctions of objects which are furnished by space and time, and the rational memory of those higher combinations which the rational faculties super induce upon those lower. The artificial memory proposes to substitute for the natural and necessary relations under which all objects must present and arrange themselves, an entirely new set of relations that are purely arbitrary and mechanical, which excite little or no other interest than that they are to aid us in remembering. It follows that if the mind tasks itself to the special effort of considering objects under these artificial relations, it will give less attention to those which have a direct and legitimate interest for itself." Granville says: "The defects of most methods which have been devised and employed for improving the memory, lies in the fact that while they serve to impress particular subjects on the mind, they do not render the memory, as a whole, ready or attentive." Fuller says: "Surely an art of memory may be made more destructive to natural memory than spectacles are to eyes." These opinions of the best authorities might be multiplied indefinitely—the consensus of the best opinion is decidedly against the artificial systems, and in favour of the natural ones.

Natural systems of memory culture are based upon the fundamental conception so well expressed by Helvetius, several centuries ago, when he said: "The extent of the memory depends, first, on the daily use we make of it; secondly, upon the attention with which we consider the objects we would impress upon it; and, thirdly, upon the order in which we range our ideas." This then is the list of the three essentials in the cultivation of the memory: (1) Use and exercise; review and practice; (2) Attention and Interest; and (3) Intelligent Association.

You will find that in the several chapters of this book dealing with the various phases of memory, we urge, first, last, and all the time, the importance of the use and employment of the memory, in the way of employment, exercise, practice and review work. Like any other mental faculty, or physical function, the memory will tend to atrophy by disuse, and increase, strengthen and develop by rational exercise and employment within the bounds of moderation. You develop a muscle by exercise; you train any special faculty of the mind in the same way; and you must pursue the same method in the case of the memory, if you would develop it. Nature's laws are constant, and bear a close analogy to each other. You will also notice the great stress that we lay upon the use of the faculty of attention, accompanied by interest. By attention you acquire the impressions that you file away in your mental record-file of memory. And the degree of attention regulates the depth, clearness and strength of the impression. Without a good record, you cannot expect to obtain a good reproduction of it. A poor phonographic record results in a poor reproduction, and the rule applies in the case of the memory as well. You will also notice that we explain the laws of association, and the principles which govern the subject, as well as the methods whereby the proper associations may be made. Every association that you weld to an idea or an impression, serves as a cross-reference in the index, whereby the thing is found by remembrance or recollection when it is needed. We call your attention to the fact that one's entire education depends for its efficiency upon this law of association. It is a most important feature in the rational cultivation of the memory, while at the same time being the bane of the artificial systems. Natural associations educate, while artificial ones tend to weaken the powers of the mind, if carried to any great length.

There is no Royal Road to Memory. The cultivation of the memory depends upon the practice along certain scientific lines according to well established psychological laws. Those who hope for a sure "short cut" will be disappointed, for none such exists. As Halleck says: "The student ought not to be disappointed to find that memory is no exception to the rule of improvement by proper methodical and long continued exercise. There is no royal road, no short cut, to the improvement of either mind or muscle. But the student who follows the rules which psychology has laid down may know that he is walking in the shortest path, and not wandering aimlessly about. Using these rules, he will advance much faster than those without chart, compass, or pilot. He will find mnemonics of extremely limited use. Improvement comes by orderly steps. Methods that dazzle at first sight never give solid results."

The student is urged to pay attention to what we have to say in other chapters of the book upon the subjects of attention and association. It is not necessary to state here the particulars that we mention there. The cultivation of the attention is a prerequisite for good memory, and deficiency in this respect means deficiency not only in the field of memory but also in the general field of mental work. In all branches of The New Psychology there is found a constant repetition of the injunction to cultivate the faculty of attention and concentration. Halleck says: "Haziness of perception lies at the root of many a bad memory. If perception is definite, the first step has been taken toward insuring a good memory. If the first impression is vivid, its effect upon the brain cells is more lasting. All persons ought to practice their visualizing power. This will react upon perception and make it more definite. Visualizing will also form a brain habit of remembering things pictorially, and hence more exactly."

The subject of association must also receive its proper share of attention, for it is by means of association that the stored away records of the memory may be recovered or re-collected. As Blackie says: "Nothing helps the mind so much as order and classification. Classes are few, individuals many: to know the class well is to know what is most essential in the character of the individual, and what burdens the memory least to retain." And as Halleck says regarding the subject of association by relation: "Whenever we can discover any relation between facts, it is far easier to remember them. The intelligent law of memory may be summed up in these words: Endeavor to link by some thought relation each new mental acquisition to an old one. Bind new facts to other facts by relations of similarity, cause and effect, whole and part, or by any logical relation, and we shall find that when an idea occurs to us, a host of related ideas will flow into the mind. If we wish to prepare a speech or write an article on any subject, pertinent illustrations will suggest themselves. The person whose memory is merely contiguous will wonder how we think of them."

In your study for the cultivation of the memory, along the lines laid down in this book, you have read the first chapter thereof and have informed yourself thoroughly regarding the importance of the memory to the individual, and what a large part it plays in the entire work of the mind. Now carefully read the third chapter and acquaint yourself with the possibilities in the direction of cultivating the memory to a high degree, as evidenced by the instances related of the extreme case of development noted therein. Then study the chapter on memory systems, and realize that the only true method is the natural method, which requires work, patience and practice—then make up your mind that you will follow this plan as far as it will take you. Then acquaint yourself with the secret of memory—the subconscious region of the mind, in which the records of memory are kept, stored away and indexed, and in which the little mental office-boys are busily at work. This will give you the key to the method. Then take up the two chapters on attention, and association, respectively, and acquaint yourself with these important principles. Then study the chapter on the phases of memory, and take mental stock of yourself, determining in which phase of memory you are strongest, and in which you need development. Then read the two chapters on training the eye and ear, respectively—you need this instruction. Then read over the several chapters on the training of the special phases of the memory, whether you need them or not—you may find something of importance in them. Then read the concluding chapter, which gives you some general advice and parting instruction. Then return to the chapters dealing with the particular phases of memory in which you have decided to develop yourself, studying the details of the instruction carefully until you know every point of it. Then, most important of all—*get to work*. The rest is a matter of practice, practice, practice, and rehearsal. Go back to the chapters from time to time, and refresh your mind regarding the details. Re-read each chapter at intervals. Make the book your own, in every sense of the word, by absorbing its contents.

Chapter 3

Celebrated Cases of Memory

In order that the student may appreciate the marvellous extent of development possible to the memory, we have thought it advisable to mention a number of celebrated cases, past and present. In so doing we have no desire to hold up these cases as worthy of imitation, for they are exceptional and not necessary in everyday life. We mention them merely to show to what wonderful extent development along these lines is possible.

In India, in the past, the sacred books were committed to memory, and handed down from teacher to student, for ages. And even today it is not uncommon thing for the student to be able to repeat, word for word, some voluminous religious work equal in extent to the New Testament. Max Muller states that the entire text and glossary of Panini's Sanscrit grammar, equal in extent to the entire Bible, were handed down orally for several centuries before being committed to writing. There are Brahmins to-day who have committed to memory, and who can repeat at will, the entire collection of religious poems known as the *Mahabarata*, consisting of over 300,000 *slokas* or verses. Leland states that, "the Slavonian minstrels of the present day have by heart with remarkable accuracy immensely long epic poems. I have found the same among Algonquin Indians whose sagas or mythic legends are interminable, and yet are committed word by word accurately. I have heard in England of a lady ninety years of age whose memory was miraculous, and of which extraordinary instances are narrated by her friends. She attributed it to the fact that when young she had been made to learn a verse from the Bible every-day, and then constantly review it. As her memory improved, she learned more, the result being that in the end she could repeat from memory any verse or chapter called for in the whole Scripture."

It is related that Mithridates, the ancient warrior-king, knew the name of every soldier in his great army, and conversed fluently in twenty-two dialects. Pliny relates that Charmides could repeat the contents of every book in his large library. Hortensius, the Roman orator, had a remarkable memory which enabled him to retain and recollect the exact words of his opponent's argument, without making a single notation. On a wager, he attended a great auction sale which lasted over an entire day, and then called off in their proper order every object sold, the name of its purchaser, and the price thereof. Seneca is said to have acquired the ability to memorize several thousand proper names, and to repeat them in the order in which they had been given him, and also to reverse the order and call off the list backward. He also accomplished the feat of listening to several hundred persons, each of whom gave him a verse; memorizing the same as they proceeded; and then repeating them word for word in the exact order of their delivery—and then reversing the process, with complete success. Eusebius stated that only the memory of Esdras saved the Hebrew Scriptures to the world, for when the Chaldeans destroyed the manuscripts Esdras was able to repeat them, word by word to the scribes, who then reproduced them. The Mohammedan scholars are able to repeat the entire text of the Koran, letter perfect. Scaliger committed the entire text of the Iliad and the Odyssey, in three weeks. Ben Jonson is said to have been able to repeat all of his own works from memory, with the greatest ease.

Bulwer could repeat the Odes of Horace from memory. Pascal could repeat the entire Bible, from beginning to end, as well as being able to recall any given paragraph, verse, line, or chapter. Landor is said to have read a book but once, when he would dispose of it, having impressed it upon his memory, to be recalled years after, if necessary. Byron could recite all of his own poems. Buffon could repeat his works from beginning to end. Bryant possessed the same ability to repeat his own works. Bishop Saunderson could repeat the greater part of Juvenal and Perseus, all of Tully, and all of Horace. Fedosova, a Russian peasant, could repeat over 25,000 poems, folk-songs, legends, fairy-tales, war stories, etc., when she was over seventy years of age. The celebrated "Blind Alick," an aged Scottish beggar, could repeat any verse in the Bible called for, as well as the entire text of all the chapters and books. The newspapers, a few years ago, contained the accounts of a man named Clark who lived in New York City. He is said to have been able to give the exact presidential vote in each State of the Union since the first election. He could give the population in every town of any size in the world either present or in the past providing there was a record of the same. He could quote from Shakespeare for hours at a time beginning at any given point in any play. He could recite the entire text of the Iliad in the original Greek.

The historical case of the unnamed Dutchman is known to all students of memory. This man is said to have been able to take up a fresh newspaper; to read it all through, including the advertisements; and then to repeat its contents, word for word, from beginning to end. On one occasion he is said to have heaped wonder upon wonder, by repeating the contents of the paper backward, beginning with the last word and ending with the first. Lyon, the English actor, is said to have duplicated this feat, using a large London paper and including the market quotations, reports of the debates in Parliament, the railroad time-tables and the advertisements. A London waiter is said to have performed a similar feat, on a wager, he memorizing and correctly repeating the contents of an eight-page paper. One of the most remarkable instances of extraordinary memory known to history is that of the child Christian Meinecken. When less than four years of age he could repeat the entire Bible; two hundred hymns; five thousand Latin words; and much ecclesiastical history, theory, dogmas, arguments; and an encyclopædic quantity of theological literature. He is said to have practically retained every word that was read to him. His case was abnormal, and he died at an early age.

John Stuart Mill is said to have acquired a fair knowledge of Greek, at the age of three years, and to have memorized Hume, Gibbon, and other historians, at the age of eight. Shortly after he mastered and memorized Herodotus, Xenophon, some of Socrates, and six of Plato's "Dialogues." Richard Porson is said to have memorized the entire text of Homer, Horace, Cicero, Virgil, Livy, Shakespeare, Milton, and Gibbon. He is said to have been able to memorize any ordinary novel at one careful reading; and to have several times performed the feat of memorizing the entire contents of some English monthly review.

De Rossi was able to perform the feat of repeating a hundred lines from any of the four great Italian poets, provided he was given a line at random from their works—his hundred lines following immediately after the given line. Of course this feat required the memorizing of the entire works of those poets, and the ability to take up the repetition from any given point, the latter feature being as remarkable as the former. There have been cases of printers being able to repeat, word for word, books of which they had set the type. Professor Lawson was able to teach his classes on the Scriptures without referring to the book. He claimed that if the entire stock of Bibles were to be destroyed, he could restore the book entire, from his memory.

Rev. Thomas Fuller is said to have been able to walk down a long London street, reading the names of the signs on both sides; then recalling them in the order in which they had been seen, and then by reversing the order. There are many cases on record of persons who memorized the words of every known tongue of civilization, as well as a great number of dialects, languages, and tongues of savage races. Bossuet had memorized the entire Bible, and Homer, Horace and Virgil beside. Niebuhr, the historian, was once employed in a government office, the records of which were destroyed. He, thereupon, restored the entire contents of the book of records which he had written—all from his memory. Asa Gray knew the names of ten thousand plants. Milton had a vocabulary of twenty thousand words, and Shakespeare one of twenty-five thousand. Cuvier and Agassiz are said to have memorized lists of several thousand species and varieties of animals. Magliabechi, the librarian of Florence, is said to have known the location of every volume in the large library of which he was in charge; and the complete list of works along certain lines in all the other great libraries.

He once claimed that he was able to repeat titles of over a half-million of books in many languages, and upon many subjects.

In nearly every walk of life are to be found persons with memories wonderfully developed along the lines of their particular occupation. Librarians possess this faculty to an unusual degree. Skilled workers in the finer lines of manufacture also manifest a wonderful memory for the tiny parts of the manufactured article, etc. Bank officers have a wonderful memory for names and faces. Some lawyers are able to recall cases quoted in the authorities, years after they have read them. Perhaps the most common, and yet the most remarkable, instances of memorizing in one's daily work is to be found in the cases of the theatrical profession. In some cases members of stock companies must not only be able to repeat the lines of the play they are engaged in acting at the time, but also the one that they are rehearsing for the following week, and possibly the one for the second week. And in repertoire companies the actors are required to be "letter-perfect" in a dozen or more plays—surely a wonderful feat, and yet one so common that no notice is given to it.

In some of the celebrated cases, the degree of recollection manifested is undoubtedly abnormal, but in the majority of the cases it may be seen that the result has been obtained only by the use of natural methods and persistent exercise. That wonderful memories may be acquired by anyone who will devote to the task patience, time and work, is a fact generally acknowledged by all students of the subject. It is not a *gift*, but something to be won by effort and work along scientific lines.

Chapter 4

Memory Systems

The subject of Memory Development is not a new one by any means. For two thousand years, at least, there has been much thought devoted to the subject; many books written thereupon; and many methods or "systems" invented, the purpose of which has been the artificial training of the memory. Instead of endeavoring to develop the memory by scientific training and rational practice and exercise along natural lines, there seems to have always been an idea that one could improve on Nature's methods, and that a plan might be devised by the use of some "trick" the memory might be taught to give up her hidden treasures. The law of Association has been used in the majority of these systems, often to a ridiculous degree. Fanciful systems have been built up, all artificial in their character and nature, the use of which to any great extent is calculated to result in a decrease of the natural powers of remembrance and recollection, just as in the case of natural "aids" to the physical system there is always found a decrease in the natural powers. Nature prefers to do her own work, unaided. She may be trained, led, directed and harnessed, but she insists upon doing the work herself, or dropping the task. The principle of Association is an important one, and forms a part of natural memory training, and should be so used. But when pressed into service in many of the artificial systems, the result is the erection of a complex and unnatural mental mechanism which is no more an improvement upon the natural methods, than a wooden leg is an improvement upon the original limb. There are many points in some of these "systems" which may be employed to advantage in natural memory training, by divorcing them from their fantastic rules and complex arrangement. We ask you to run over the list of the principal "systems" with us, that you may discard the useless material by recognizing it as such; and cull the valuable for your own use.

The ancient Greeks were fond of memory systems. Simonides, the Greek poet who lived about 500 B.C. was one of the early authorities, and his work has influenced nearly all of the many memory systems that have sprung up since that time. There is a romantic story connected with the foundation of his system. It is related that the poet was present at a large banquet attended by some of the principal men of the place. He was called out by a message from home, and left before the close of the meal. Shortly after he left, the ceiling of the banquet hall fell upon the guests, killing all present in the room, and mutilating their bodies so terribly that their friends were unable to recognize them. Simonides, having a well-developed memory for places and position, was able to recall the exact order in which each guest had been seated, and therefore was able to aid in the identification of the remains. This occurrence impressed him so forcibly that he devised a system of memory based upon the idea of position, which attained great popularity in Greece, and the leading writers of the day highly recommended it.

The system of Simonides was based upon the idea of position—it was known as "the topical system." His students were taught to picture in the mind a large building divided into sections, and then into rooms, halls, etc. The thing to be remembered was "visualized" as occupying some certain space or place in that building, the grouping being made according to association and resemblance. When one wished to recall the things to consciousness, all that was necessary was to visualize the mental building and then take an imaginary trip from room to room, calling off the various things as they had been placed. The Greeks thought very highly of this plan, and many variations of it were employed. Cicero said: "By those who would improve the memory, certain places must be fixed upon, and of those things which they desire to keep in memory symbols must be conceived in the mind and ranged, as it were, in those places; thus, the order of places would preserve the order of things, and the symbols of the things would denote the things themselves; so that we should use the places as waxen tablets and the symbols as letters." Quintillian advises students to "fix in their minds places of the greatest possible extent, diversified by considerable variety, such as a large house, for example, divided into many apartments. Whatever is remarkable in it is carefully impressed on the mind, so that the thought may run over every part of it without hesitation or delay... Places we must have, either fancied or selected, and images or symbols which we may invent at pleasure. These symbols are marks by which we may distinguish the particulars which we have to get by heart."

Many modern systems have been erected upon the foundation of Simonides and in some of which cases students have been charged high prices "for the secret." The following outline given by Kay gives the "secret" of many a high priced system of this class: "Select a number of rooms, and divide the walls and floor of each, in imagination, into nine equal parts or squares, three in a row. On the front wall—that opposite the entrance—of the first room, are the units; on the right-hand wall the tens; on the left hand the twenties; on the fourth wall the thirties; and on the floor the forties. Numbers 10, 20, 30 and 40, each find a place on the roof above their respective walls, while 50 occupies the centre of the room. One room will thus furnish 50 places, and ten rooms as many as 500. Having fixed these clearly in the mind, so as to be able readily and at once to tell exactly the position of each place or number, it is then necessary to associate with each of them some familiar object (or symbol) so that the object being suggested its place may be instantly remembered, or when the place be before the mind its object may immediately spring up. When this has been done thoroughly, the objects can be run over in any order from beginning to end, or from end to beginning, or the place of any particular one can at once be given. All that is further necessary is to associate the ideas we wish to remember with the objects in the various places, by which means they are easily remembered, and can be gone over in any order. In this way one may learn to repeat several hundred disconnected words or ideas in any order after hearing them only once." We do not consider it necessary to argue in detail the fact that this system is artificial and cumbersome to a great degree. While the idea of "position" may be employed to some advantage in grouping together in the memory several associated facts, ideas, or words, still the idea of employing a process such as the above in the ordinary affairs of life is ridiculous, and any system based upon it has a value only as a curiosity, or a mental acrobatic feat.

Akin to the above is the idea underlying many other "systems," and "secret methods"—the idea of Contiguity, in which words are strung together by fanciful connecting links. Feinagle describes this underlying idea, or principle, as follows: "The recollection of them is assisted by associating some idea of relation between the two; and as we find by experience that whatever is ludicrous is calculated to make a strong impression on the mind, the more ridiculous the association is the better." The systems founded upon this idea may be employed to repeat a long string of disconnected words, and similar things, but have but little practical value, notwithstanding the high prices charged for them. They serve merely as curiosities, or methods of performing "tricks" to amuse one's friends. Dr. Kothe, a German teacher, about the middle of the nineteenth century founded this last school of memory training, his ideas serving as the foundation for many teachers of high-priced "systems" or "secret methods" since that time. The above description of Feinagle gives the key to the principle employed. The working of the principle is accomplished by the employment of "intermediates" or "correlatives" as they are called; for instance, the words "chimney" and "leaf" would be connected as follows: "*Chimney*—smoke—wood—tree—*Leaf*."

Then there are systems or methods based on the old principle of the "Figure Alphabet," in which one is taught to remember dates by associating them with letters or words. For instance, one of the teachers of this class of systems, wished his pupils to remember the year 1480 by the word "BiG RaT," the capitals representing the figures in the date. Comment is unnecessary!

The student will find that nearly all the "systems" or "secret methods" that are being offered for sale in "courses," often at a very high price, are merely variations, improvements upon, or combinations of the three forms of artificial methods named above. New changes are constantly being worked on these old plans; new tunes played on the same old instruments; new chimes sounded from the same old bells. And the result is ever the same, in these cases—disappointment and disgust. There are a few natural systems on the market, nearly all of which contain information and instruction that makes them worth the price at which they are sold. As for the others—well, judge for yourself after purchasing them, if you so desire.

Regarding these artificial and fanciful systems, Kay says: "All such systems for the improvement of the memory belong to what we have considered the first or lowest form of it. They are for the most part based on light or foolish associations which have little foundation in nature, and are hence of little practical utility; and they do not tend to improve or strengthen the memory as a whole." Bacon says that these systems are "barren and useless," adding: "For immediately to repeat a multitude of names or words once repeated before, I esteem no more than rope-dancing, antic postures, and feats of activity; and, indeed, they are nearly the same things, the one being the abuse of the bodily as the other of the mental powers; and though they may cause admiration, they cannot be highly esteemed." And as another authority has said: "The systems of mnemonics as taught, are no better than crutches, useful to those who cannot walk, but impediments and hindrances to those who have the use of their limbs, and who only require to exercise them properly in order to have the full use of them."

In this work, there shall be no attempt to teach any of these "trick systems" that the student may perform for the amusement of his friends. Instead, there is only the desire to aid in developing the power to receive impressions, to register them upon the memory, and readily to reproduce them at will, naturally and easily. The lines of natural mental action will be followed throughout. The idea of this work is not to teach how one may perform "feats" of memory; but, instead, to instruct in the intelligent and practical use of the memory in the affairs of every-day life and work.

Chapter 5

The Subconscious Record-File

The old writers on the subject were wont to consider the memory as a separate faculty of the mind, but this idea disappeared before the advancing tide of knowledge which resulted in the acceptance of the conception now known as The New Psychology. This new conception recognizes the existence of a vast "out of consciousness" region of the mind, one phase of which is known as the subconscious mind, or the subconscious field of mental activities. In this field of mentation the activities of memory have their seat. A careful consideration of the subject brings the certainty that the entire work of the memory is performed in this subconscious region of the mind. Only when the subconscious record is represented to the conscious field, and recollection or remembrance results, does the memorized idea or impression emerge from the subconscious region. An understanding of this fact simplifies the entire subject of the memory, and enables us to perfect plans and methods whereby the memory may be developed, improved and trained, by means of the direction of the subconscious activities by the use of the conscious faculties and the will.

Hering says: "Memory is a faculty not only of our conscious states, but also, and much more so, of our unconscious ones." Kay says: "It is impossible to understand the true nature of memory, or how to train it aright, unless we have a clear conception of the fact that there is much in the mind of which we are unconscious... The highest form of memory, as of all the mental powers, is the unconscious—when what we wish to recall comes to us spontaneously, without any conscious thought or search for it. Frequently when we wish to recall something that has previously been in the mind we are unable to do so by any conscious effort of the will; but we turn the attention to something else, and after a time the desired information comes up spontaneously when we are not consciously thinking of it." Carpenter says: "There is the working of a mechanism beneath the consciousness which, when once set going, runs on of itself, and which is more likely to evolve the desired result when the conscious activity of the mind is exerted in a direction altogether different."

This subconscious region of the mind is the great record-file of everything we have ever experienced, thought or known. Everything is recorded there. The best authorities now generally agree that there is no such thing as an absolute forgetting of even the most minute impression, notwithstanding the fact that we may be unable to recollect or remember it, owing to its faintness, or lack of associated "indexing." It is held that everything is to be found in that subconscious index-file, if we can only manage to find its place. Kay says: "In like manner we believe that every impression or thought that has once been before consciousness remains ever afterward impressed upon the mind.

It may never again come up before consciousness, but it will doubtless remain in that vast ultra-conscious region of the mind, unconsciously moulding and fashioning our subsequent thoughts and actions. It is only a small part of what exists in the mind that we are conscious of. There is always much that is known to be in the mind that exists in it unconsciously, and must be stored away somewhere. We may be able to recall it into consciousness when we wish to do so; but at other times the mind is unconscious of its existence. Further, every one's experience must tell him that there is much in his mind that he cannot always recall when he may wish to do so,—much that he can recover only after a labored search, or that he may search for in vain at the time, but which may occur to him afterwards when perhaps he is not thinking about it. Again, much that we probably would never be able to recall, or that would not recur to us under ordinary circumstances, we may remember to have had in the mind when it is mentioned to us by others. In such a case there must still have remained some trace or scintilla of it in the mind before we could recognize it as having been there before."

Morell says: "We have every reason to believe that mental power when once called forth follows the analogy of everything we see in the material universe in the fact of its perpetuity. Every single effort of mind is a creation which can never go back again into nonentity. It may slumber in the depths of forgetfulness as light and heat slumber in the coal seams, but there it is, ready at the bidding of some appropriate stimulus to come again out of the darkness into the light of consciousness." Beattie says: "That which has been long forgotten, nay, that which we have often in vain endeavored to recollect, will sometimes without an effort of ours occur to us on a sudden, and, if I may so speak, of its own accord." Hamilton says:

"The mind frequently contains whole systems of knowledge which, though in our normal state they may have faded into absolute oblivion, may in certain abnormal states, as madness, delirium, somnambulism, catalepsy, etc., flash out into luminous consciousness... For example, there are cases in which the extinct memory of whole languages were suddenly restored." Lecky says: "It is now fully established that a multitude of events which are so completely forgotten that no effort of the will can revive them, and that the statement of them calls up no reminiscences, may nevertheless be, so to speak, embedded in the memory, and may be reproduced with intense vividness under certain physical conditions."

In proof of the above, the authorities give many instances recorded in scientific annals. Coleridge relates the well-known case of the old woman who could neither read nor write, who when in the delirium of fever incessantly recited in very pompous tones long passages from the Latin, Greek and Hebrew, with a distinct enunciation and precise rendition. Notes of her ravings were taken down by shorthand, and caused much wonderment, until it was afterwards found that in her youth she had been employed as a servant in the house of a clergyman who was in the habit of walking up and down in his study reading aloud from his favourite classical and religious writers. In his books were found marked passages corresponding to the notes taken from the girl's ravings. Her subconscious memory had stored up the sounds of these passages heard in her early youth, but of which she had no recollection in her normal state. Beaufort, describing his sensations just before being rescued from drowning says: "Every incident of my former life seemed to glance across my recollection in a retrograde procession, not in mere outline, but in a picture filled with every minute and collateral feature, thus forming a panoramic view of my whole existence."

Kay truly observes: "By adopting the opinion that every thought or impression that had once been consciously before the mind is ever afterwards retained, we obtain light on many obscure mental phenomena; and especially do we draw from it the conclusion of the perfectibility of the memory to an almost unlimited extent. We cannot doubt that, could we penetrate to the lowest depths of our mental nature, we should there find traces of every impression we have received, every thought we have entertained, and every act we have done through our past life, each one making its influence felt in the way of building up our present knowledge, or in guiding our every-day actions; and if they persist in the mind, might it not be possible to recall most if not all of them into consciousness when we wished to do so, if our memories or powers of recollection were what they should be?"

As we have said, this great subconscious region of the mind—this Memory region—may be thought of as a great record file, with an intricate system of indexes, and office boys whose business it is to file away the records; to index them; and to find them when needed. The records record only what we have impressed upon them by the attention, the degree of depth and clearness depending entirely upon the degree of attention which we bestowed upon the original impression. We can never expect to have the office boys of the memory bring up anything that they have not been given to file away. The indexing, and cross-references are supplied by the association existing between the various impressions. The more cross-references, or associations that are connected with an idea, thought or impression that is filed away in the memory, the greater the chances of it being found readily when wanted. These two features of attention and association, and the parts they play in the phenomena of memory, are mentioned in detail in other chapters of this book.

These little office boys of the memory are an industrious and willing lot of little chaps, but like all boys they do their best work when kept in practice. Idleness and lack of exercise cause them to become slothful and careless, and forgetful of the records under their charge. A little fresh exercise and work soon take the cobwebs out of their brains, and they spring eagerly to their tasks. They become familiar with their work when exercised properly, and soon become very expert. They have a tendency to remember, on their own part, and when a certain record is called for often they grow accustomed to its place, and can find it without referring to the indexes at all. But their trouble comes from faint and almost illegible records, caused by poor attention—these they can scarcely decipher when they do succeed in finding them. Lack of proper indexing by associations causes them much worry and extra work, and sometimes they are unable to find the records at all from this neglect. Often, however, after they have told you that they could not find a thing, and you have left the place in disgust, they will continue their search and hours afterward will surprise you by handing you the desired idea, or impression, which they had found carelessly indexed or improperly filed away. In these chapters you will be helped, if you will carry in your mind these little office boys of the memory record file, and the hard work they have to do for you, much of which is made doubly burdensome by your own neglect and carelessness. Treat these little fellows right and they will work overtime for you, willingly and joyfully. But they need your assistance and encouragement, and an occasional word of praise and commendation.

Chapter 6

Attention

As we have seen in the preceding chapters, before one can expect to recall or remember a thing, that thing must have been impressed upon the records of his subconsciousness, distinctly and clearly. And the main factor of the recording of impressions is that quality of the mind that we call Attention. All the leading authorities on the subject of memory recognize and teach the value of attention in the cultivation and development of the memory. Tupper says: "Memory, the daughter of Attention, is the teeming mother of wisdom." Lowell says: "Attention is the stuff that Memory is made of, and Memory is accumulated Genius." Hall says: "In the power of fixing the attention lies the most precious of the intellectual habits." Locke says: "When the ideas that offer themselves are taken notice of, and, as it were, registered in the memory, it is Attention." Stewart says: "The permanence of the impression which anything leaves on the memory, is proportionate to the degree of attention which was originally given to it." Thompson says: "The experiences most permanently impressed upon consciousness are those upon which the greatest amount of attention has been fixed." Beattie says: "The force wherewith anything strikes the mind is generally in proportion to the degree of attention bestowed upon it. The great art of memory is attention... Inattentive people have always bad memories." Kay says: "It is generally held by philosophers that without some degree of attention no impression of any duration could be made on the mind, or laid up in the memory." Hamilton says: "It is a law of the mind that the intensity of the present consciousness determines the vivacity of the future memory; memory and consciousness are thus in the direct ratio of each other. Vivid consciousness, long memory; faint consciousness, short memory; no consciousness, no memory... An act of attention, that is an act of concentration, seems thus necessary to every exertion of consciousness, as a certain contraction of the pupil is requisite to every exertion of vision. Attention, then, is to consciousness what the contraction of the pupil is to sight, or to the eye of the mind what the microscope or telescope is to the bodily eye. It constitutes the better half of all intellectual power."

We have quoted from the above authorities at considerable length, for the purpose of impressing upon your mind the importance of this subject of Attention. The subconscious regions of the mind are the great storehouses of the mental records of impressions from within and without. Its great systems of filing, recording and indexing these records constitute that which we call memory. But before any of this work is possible, impressions must first have been received. And, as you may see from the quotations just given, these impressions depend upon the power of attention given to the things making the impressions. If there has been given great attention, there will be clear and deep impressions; if there has been given but average attention, there will be but average impressions; if there has been given but faint attention, there will be but faint impressions; if there has been given no attention, there will be no records.

One of the most common causes of poor attention is to be found in the lack of interest. We are apt to remember the things in which we have been most interested, because in that outpouring of interest there has been a high degree of attention manifested. A man may have a very poor memory for many things, but when it comes to the things in which his interest is involved he often remembers the most minute details. What is called involuntary attention is that form of attention that follows upon interest, curiosity, or desire—no special effort of the will being required in it. What is called voluntary attention is that form of attention that is bestowed upon objects not necessarily interesting, curious, or attractive—this requires the application of the will, and is a mark of a developed character. Every person has more or less involuntary attention, while but few possess developed voluntary attention. The former is instinctive—the latter comes only by practice and training.

But there is this important point to be remembered, that *interest may be developed by voluntary attention* bestowed and held upon an object. Things that are originally lacking in sufficient interest to attract the involuntary attention may develop a secondary interest if the voluntary attention be placed upon and held upon them. As Halleck says on this point: "When it is said that attention will not take a firm hold on an uninteresting thing, we must not forget that anyone not shallow and fickle can soon discover something interesting in most objects. Here cultivated minds show their especial superiority, for the attention which they are able to give generally ends in finding a pearl in the most uninteresting looking oyster. When an object necessarily loses interest from one point of view, such minds discover in it new attributes. The essence of genius is to present an old thing in new ways, whether it be some force in nature or some aspect of humanity."

It is very difficult to teach another person how to cultivate the attention. This because the whole thing consists so largely in the use of the will, and by faithful practice and persistent application. The first requisite is *the determination to use the will.* You must argue it out with yourself, until you become convinced that it is necessary and desirable for you to acquire the art of voluntary attention—you must convince yourself beyond reasonable doubt. This is the first step and one more difficult than it would seem at first sight. The principal difficulty in it lies in the fact that to do the thing you must do some active earnest thinking, and the majority of people are too lazy to indulge in such mental effort. Having mastered this first step, you must induce a strong burning desire to acquire the art of voluntary attention—you must learn to want it hard. In this way you induce a condition of interest and attractiveness where it was previously lacking. Third and last, you must hold your will firmly and persistently to the task, and practice faithfully.

Begin by turning your attention upon some uninteresting thing and studying its details until you are able to describe them. This will prove very tiresome at first but you must stick to it. Do not practice too long at a time at first; take a rest and try it again later. You will soon find that it comes easier, and that a new interest is beginning to manifest itself in the task. Examine this book, as practice, learn how many pages there are in it; how many chapters; how many pages in each chapter; the details of type, printing and binding—all the little things about it—so that you could give another person a full account of the minor details of the book. This may seem uninteresting—and so it will be at first—but a little practice will create a new interest in the petty details, and you will be surprised at the number of little things that you will notice. This plan, practiced on many things, in spare hours, will develop the power of voluntary attention and perception in anyone, no matter how deficient he may have been in these things. If you can get someone else to join in the game-task with you, and then each endeavor to excel the other in finding details, the task will be much easier, and better work will be accomplished. Begin to take notice of things about you; the places you visit; the things in the rooms, etc. In this way you will start the habit of "noticing things," which is the first requisite for memory development.

Halleck gives the following excellent advice on this subject: "To look at a thing intelligently is the most difficult of all arts. The first rule for the cultivation of accurate perception is: Do not try to perceive the whole of a complex object at once. Take the human face as an example. A man, holding an important position to which he had been elected, offended many people because he could not remember faces, and hence failed to recognize individuals the second time he met them. His trouble was in looking at the countenance as a whole. When he changed his method of observation, and noticed carefully the nose, mouth, eyes, chin, and color of hair, he at once began to find recognition easier. He was no longer in difficulty of mistaking A for B, since he remembered that the shape of B's nose was different, or the color of his hair at least three shades lighter. This example shows that another rule can be formulated: Pay careful attention to details. We are perhaps asked to give a minute description of the exterior of a somewhat noted suburban house that we have lately seen. We reply in general terms, giving the size and color of the house. Perhaps we also have an idea of part of the material used in the exterior construction. We are asked to be exact about the shape of the door, porch, roof, chimneys and windows; whether the windows are plain or circular, whether they have cornices, or whether the trimmings around them are of the same material as the rest of the house. A friend, who will be unable to see the house, wishes to know definitely about the angles of the roof, and the way the windows are arranged with reference to them. Unless we can answer these questions exactly, we merely tantalize our friends by telling them we have seen the house. To see an object merely as an undiscriminated mass of something in a certain place, is to do no more than a donkey accomplishes as he trots along."

There are three general rules that may be given in this matter of bestowing the voluntary attention in the direction of actually *seeing* things, instead of merely looking at them. The first is: Make yourself take an interest in the thing. The second: See it as if you were taking note of it in order to repeat its details to a friend—this will force you to "take notice." The third: Give to your subconsciousness a mental command to take note of what you are looking at—say to it; "Here, you take note of this and remember it for me!" This last consists of a peculiar "knack" that can be attained by a little practice—it will "come to you" suddenly after a few trials.

Regarding this third rule whereby the subconsciousness is made to work for you, Charles Leland has the following to say, although he uses it to illustrate another point: "As I understand it, it is a kind of impulse or projection of will into the coming work. I may here illustrate this with a curious fact in physics. If the reader wished to ring a doorbell so as to produce as much sound as possible, he would probably pull it as far back as he could, and then let it go. But if he would, in letting it go, simply give it a tap with his forefinger, he would actually redouble the sound. Or, to shoot an arrow as far as possible, it is not enough to *merely* draw the bow to its utmost span or tension. If, just as it goes, you will give the bow a quick push, though the effort be trifling, the arrow will fly almost as far again as it would have done without it. Or, if, as is well known in wielding a very sharp sabre, we make the draw cut; that is, if to the blow or chop, as with an axe, we also add a certain slight pull, simultaneously, we can cut through a silk handkerchief or a sheep. Forethought (command to the subconsciousness) is the tap on the bell; the push on the bow; the draw on the sabre. It is the deliberate but yet rapid action of the mind when before dismissing thought, we bid the mind to consequently respond. It is more than merely thinking what we are to do; it is the bidding or ordering the Self to fulfill a task before willing it."

Remember first, last and always, that before you can remember, or recollect, you must first *perceive*; and that perception is possible only through attention, and responds in degree to the latter. Therefore, it has truly been said that: "The great Art of Memory is Attention."

Chapter 7

Association

In the preceding chapters we have seen that in order that a thing may be remembered, it must be impressed clearly upon the mind in the first place; and that in order to obtain a clear impression there must be a manifestation of attention. So much for the recording of the impressions. But when we come to recalling, recollecting or remembering the impressions we are brought face to face with another important law of memory—the law of Association. Association plays a part analogous to the indexing and cross-indexing of a book; a library; or another system in which the aim is to readily find something that has been filed away, or contained in some way in a collection of similar things. As Kay says: "In order that what is in the memory may be recalled or brought again before consciousness, it is necessary that it be regarded in connection, or in association with one or more other things or ideas, and as a rule the greater the number of other things with which it is associated the greater the likelihood of its recall. The two processes are involved in every act of memory. We must first impress, and then we must associate.

Without a clear impression being formed, that which is recalled will be indistinct and inaccurate; and unless it is associated with something else in the mind, it cannot be recalled. If we may suppose an idea existing in the mind by itself, unconnected with any other idea, its recall would be impossible."

All the best authorities recognize and teach the importance of this law of association, in connection with the memory. Abercrombie says: "Next to the effect of attention is the remarkable influence produced upon memory by association." Carpenter says: "The recording power of memory mainly depends upon the degree of attention we give to the idea to be remembered. The reproducing power again altogether depends upon the nature of the associations by which the new idea has been linked on to other ideas which have been previously recorded." Ribot says: "The most fundamental law which regulates psychological phenomena is the law of association. In its comprehensive character it is comparable to the law of attraction in the physical world." Mill says: "That which the law of gravitation is to astronomy; that which the elementary properties of the tissues are to physiology; the law of association of ideas is to psychology." Stewart says: "The connection between memory and the association of ideas is so striking that it has been supposed by some that the whole of the phenomena might be resolved into this principle. The association of ideas connects our various thoughts with each other, so as to present them to the mind in a certain order; but it presupposes the existence of those thoughts in the mind,—in other words it presupposes a faculty of retaining the knowledge which we acquire. On the other hand, it is evident that without the associating principle, the power of retaining our thoughts, and of recognizing them when they occur to us, would have been of little use; for the most important articles of our knowledge might have remained latent in the mind, even when those occasions presented themselves to which they were immediately applicable."

Association of ideas depends upon two principles known, respectively, as (1) the law of contiguity; and (2) the law of similarity. Association by contiguity is that form of association by which an idea is linked, connected, or associated with the sensation, thought, or idea immediately preceding it, and that which directly follows it. Each idea, or thought, is a link in a great chain of thought being connected with the preceding link and the succeeding link. Association by similarity is that form of association by which an idea, thought, or sensation is linked, connected, or associated with ideas, thoughts, or sensations of a similar kind, which have occurred previously or subsequently. The first form of association is the relation of sequence—the second the relation of kind.

Association by contiguity is the great law of thought, as well as of memory. As Kay says: "The great law of mental association is that of contiguity, by means of which sensations and ideas that have been in the mind together or in close succession, tend to unite together, or cohere in such a way that the one can afterward recall the other. The connection that naturally subsists between a sensation or idea in the mind, and that which immediately preceded or followed it, is of the strongest and most intimate nature. The two, strictly speaking, are but one, forming one complete thought." As Taine says: "To speak correctly, there is no isolated or separate sensation. A sensation is a state which begins as a continuation of preceding ones, and ends by losing itself in those following it; it is by an arbitrary severing, and for the convenience of language, that we set it apart as we do; its beginning is the end of another, and its ending the beginning of another." As Ribot says: "When we read or hear a sentence, for example, at the commencement of the fifth word something of the fourth word still remains. Association by contiguity may be separated into two sub-classes—contiguity in time; and contiguity in space. In contiguity in time there is manifested the tendency of the memory to recall the impressions in the same order in which they were received—the first impression suggesting the second, and that the third, and so on. In this way the child learns to repeat the alphabet, and the adult the succeeding lines of a poem. As Priestly says: "In a poem, the end of each preceding word being connected with the beginning of the succeeding one, we can easily repeat them in that order, but we are not able to repeat them backwards till they have been frequently named in that order." Memory of words, or groups of words, depends upon this form of contigious association. Some persons are able to repeat long poems from beginning to end, with perfect ease, but are unable to repeat any particular sentence, or verse, without working down to it from the beginning. Contiguity in space is manifested in forms of recollection or remembrance by "position." Thus by remembering the things connected with the position of a particular thing, we are enabled to recall the thing itself. As we have seen in a preceding chapter, some forms of memory systems have been based on this law. If you will recall some house or room in which you have been, you will find that you will remember one object after another, in the order of the relative positions, or contiguity in space, or position. Beginning with the front hall, you may travel in memory from one room to another, recalling each with the objects it contains, according to the degree of attention you bestowed upon them originally. Kay says of association by contiguity: "It is on this principle of contiguity that mnemonical systems are constructed, as when what we wish to remember is associated in the mind with a certain object or locality, the ideas associated will at once come up; or when each word or idea is associated with the one immediately preceding it, so that when the one is recalled the other comes up along with it, and thus long lists of names or long passages of books can be readily learnt by heart."

From the foregoing, it will be seen that it is of great importance that we correlate our impressions with those preceding and following. The more closely knitted together our impressions are, the more closely will they cohere, and the greater will be the facility of remembering or recollecting them. We should endeavor to form our impressions of things so that they will be associated with other impressions, in time and space. Every other thing that is associated in the mind with a given thing, serves as a "loose end" of memory, which if once grasped and followed up will lead us to the thing we desire to recall to mind.

Association by similarity is the linking together of impressions of a similar kind, irrespective of time and place. Carpenter expresses it as follows: "The law of similarity expresses the general fact that any present state of consciousness tends to revive previous states which are similar to it... Rational or philosophical association is when a fact or statement on which the attention is fixed is associated with some fact previously known, to which it has a relation, or with some subject which it is calculated to illustrate." And as Kay says: "The similars may be widely apart in space or in time, but they are brought together and associated through their resemblance to each other. Thus, a circumstance of to-day may recall circumstances of a similar nature that occurred perhaps at very different times, and they will become associated together in the mind, so that afterwards the presence of one will tend to recall the others." Abercrombie says of this phase of association: "The habit of correct association—that is, connecting facts in the mind according to their true relations, and to the manner in which they tend to illustrate each other, is one of the principle means of improving the memory, particularly that kind of memory which is an essential quality of a cultivated mind—namely, that which is founded not upon incidental connections, but on true and important relations."

As Beattie says: "The more relations or likenesses that we find or can establish between objects, the more easily will the view of one lead us to recollect the rest." And as Kay says: "In order to fix a thing in the memory, we must associate it with something in the mind already, and the more closely that which we wish to remember resembles that with which it is associated, the better is it fixed in the memory, and the more readily is it recalled. If the two strongly resemble each other, or are not to be distinguished from each other, then the association is of the strongest kind... The memory is able to retain and replace a vastly greater number of ideas, if they are associated or arranged on some principle of similarity, than if they are presented merely as isolated facts. It is not by the multitude of ideas, but they want of arrangement among them, that the memory is burdened and its powers weakened." As Arnott says: "The ignorant man may be said to have charged his hundred hooks of knowledge (to use a rude simile), with single objects, while the informed man makes each hook support a long chain to which thousands of kindred and useful things are attached."

We ask each student of this book to acquaint himself with the general idea of the working features of the law of association as given in this chapter for the reason that much of the instruction to be given under the head of the several phases and classes of memory is based upon an application of the Law of Association, in connection with the law of Attention. These fundamental principles should be clearly grasped before one proceeds to the details of practice and exercise. One should know not only "how" to use the mind and memory in certain ways, but also "why" it is to be used in that particular way. By understanding the "reason of it," one is better able to follow out the directions.

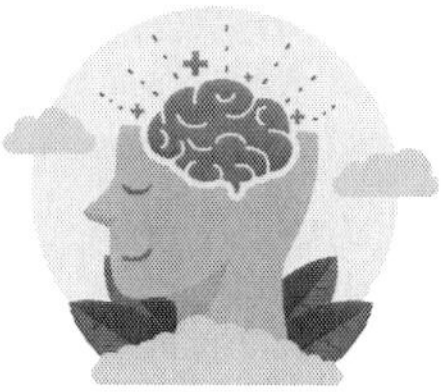

Chapter 8

Phases of Memory

One of the first things apt to be noticed by the student of memory is the fact that there are several different phases of the manifestation of memory. That is to say, that there are several general classes into which the phenomena of memory may be grouped. And accordingly we find some persons quite highly developed in certain phases of memory, and quite deficient in others. If there were but one phase or class of memory, then a person who had developed his memory along any particular line would have at the same time developed it equally along all the other lines. But this is far from being the true state of affairs. We find men who are quite proficient in recalling the impression of faces, while they find it very difficult to recall the names of the persons whose faces they remember. Others can remember faces, and not names. Others have an excellent recollection of localities, while others are constantly losing themselves. Others remember dates, prices, numbers, and figures generally, while deficient in other forms of recollection. Others remember tales, incidents, anecdotes etc., while forgetting other things. And so on, each person being apt to possess a memory good in some phases, while deficient in others.

The phases of memory may be divided into two general classes, namely (1) Memory of Sense Impressions; and (2) Memory of Ideas. This classification is somewhat arbitrary, for the reason that sense impressions develop into ideas, and ideas are composed to a considerable extent of sense impressions, but in a general way the classification serves its purpose, which is the grouping together of certain phases of the phenomena of memory.

Memory of Sense Impressions of course includes the impressions received from all of the five senses: sight; hearing; taste; touch; and smell. But when we come down to a practical examination of sense impressions retained in the memory, we find that the majority of such impressions are those obtained through the two respective senses of sight and hearing. The impressions received from the sense of taste, touch and smell, respectively, are comparatively small, except in the cases of certain experts in special lines, whose occupation consists in acquiring a very delicate sense of taste, smell or touch, and correspondingly a fine sense of memory along these particular lines. For instance, the wine-taster and tea-tasters, who are able to distinguish between the various grades of merchandise handled by them, have developed not only very fine senses of taste and smell, but also a remarkable memory of the impressions previously received, the power of discrimination depending as much upon the memory as upon the special sense. In the same way the skilled surgeon as well as the skilled mechanic acquires a fine sense of touch and a correspondingly highly developed memory of touch impressions.

But, as we have said, the greater part of the sense impressions stored away in our memories are those previously received through the senses of sight and hearing, respectively. The majority of sense impressions, stored away in the memory, have been received more or less involuntarily, that is with the application of but a slight degree of attention. They are more or less indistinct and hazy, and are recalled with difficulty, the remembrance of them generally coming about without conscious effort, according to the law of association. That is, they come principally when we are thinking about something else upon which we have given thought and attention, and with which they have been associated. There is quite a difference between the remembrance of sense impressions received in this way, and those which we record by the bestowal of attention, interest and concentration.

The sense impressions of sight are by far the most numerous in our subconscious storehouse. We are constantly exercising our sense of sight, and receiving thousands of different sight impressions every hour. But the majority of these impressions are but faintly recorded upon the memory, because we give to them but little attention or interest. But it is astonishing, at times, when we find that when we recall some important event or incident we also recall many faint sight impressions of which we did not dream we had any record. To realize the important part played by sight impressions in the phenomena of memory, recall some particular time or event in your life, and see how many more things that you *saw* are remembered, compared with the number of things that you *heard*, or tasted, or felt or smelled.

Second in number, however, are the impressions received through the sense of hearing, and consequently the memory stores away a great number of sound impressions. In some cases the impressions of sight and sound are joined together, as for instance in the case of words, in which not only the sound but the shape of the letters composing the word, or rather the word-shape itself, are stored away together, and consequently are far more readily remembered or recollected than things of which but one sense impression is recorded. Teachers of memory use this fact as a means of helping their students to memorize words by speaking them aloud, and then writing them down. Many persons memorize names in this way, the impression of the written word being added to the impression of the sound, thus doubling the record. The more impressions that you can make regarding a thing, the greater are the chances of your easily recollecting it. Likewise it is very important to attach an impression of a weaker sense, to that of a stronger one, in order that the former may be memorized. For instance, if you have a good eye memory, and a poor ear memory, it is well to attach your sound impressions to the sight impressions. And if you have a poor eye memory, and a good ear memory it is important to attach your sight impressions to your sound impressions. In this way you take advantage of the law of association, of which we have told you.

Under the sub-class of sight impressions, are found the smaller divisions of memory known as memory of locality; memory of figures; memory of form; memory of color; and memory of written or printed words. Under the sub-class of sound impressions are found the smaller divisions of memory known as memory of spoken words; memory of names; memory of stories; memory of music, etc. We shall pay special attention to these forms of memory, in succeeding chapters.

The second general class of memory,—memory of ideas,—includes the memory of facts, events, thoughts, lines of reasoning, etc., and is regarded as higher in the scale than the memory of sense impressions, although not more necessary nor useful to the average person. This form of memory of course accompanies the higher lines of intellectual effort and activities, and constitutes a large part of what is known as true education, that is education which teaches one to think instead of to merely memorize certain things taught in books or lectures.

The well-rounded man, mentally, is he who has developed his memory on all sides, rather than the one who has developed but one special phase of the faculty. It is true that a man's interest and occupation certainly tend to develop his memory according to his daily needs and requirements, but it is well that he should give to the other parts of his memory field some exercise, in order that he may not grow one-sided. As Halleck has said: "Many persons think that memory is mainly due to sight; but we have as many different kinds of memory as we have senses. To sight, the watermelon is a long greenish body, but this is its least important quality. Sight alone gives the poorest idea of the watermelon. We approach the vine where the fruit is growing, and in order to decide whether it is ripe, we tap the rind and judge by the sound. We must remember that a ripe watermelon has a certain resonance. By passing our hands over the melon, we learn that it has certain touch characteristics. We cut it open and learn the qualities of taste and smell. All this knowledge afforded by the different senses must enter into a perfected memory image. Hence we see that many complex processes go to form an idea of a thing. Napoleon was not content with only hearing a name. He wrote it down, and having satisfied his eye memory as well as his ear memory, he threw the paper away."

In this book we shall point out the methods and processes calculated to round out the memory of the student. As a rule his strong phases of memory need but little attention, although even in these a little scientific knowledge will be of use. But in the weaker phases, those phases in which his memory is "poor," he should exert a new energy and activity, to the end that these weaker regions of the memory may be cultivated and fertilized, and well stored with the seed impressions, which will bear a good crop in time. There is no phase, field, or class of memory that is not capable of being highly developed by intelligent application. It requires practice, exercise and work—but the reward is great. Many a man is handicapped by being deficient in certain phases of memory, while proficient in others. The remedy is in his own hands, and we feel that in this book we have given to each the means whereby he may acquire a "good" memory along any or all lines.

Chapter 9

Training the Eye

Before the memory can be stored with sight impressions—before the mind can recollect or remember such impressions—the eye must be used under the direction of the attention. We think that we see things when we look at them, but in reality we *see* but few things, in the sense of registering clear and distinct impressions of them upon the tablets of the subconscious mind. We *look at* them rather than *see* them.

Halleck says regarding this "sight without seeing" idea: "A body may be imaged on the retina without insuring perception. There must be an effort to concentrate the attention upon the many things which the world presents to our senses. A man once said to the pupils of a large school, all of whom had seen cows: 'I should like to find out how many of you know whether a cow's ears are above, below, behind, or in front of her horns. I want only those pupils to raise their hands who are sure about the position and who will promise to give a dollar to charity if they answer wrong.' Only two hands were raised. Their owners had drawn cows and in order to do that had been forced to concentrate their attention upon the animals. Fifteen pupils were sure that they had seen cats climb trees and descend them. There was unanimity of opinion that the cats went up heads first. When asked whether the cats came down head or tail first, the majority were sure that the cats descended as they were never known to do. Anyone who had ever noticed the shape of the laws of any beast of prey could have answered the question without seeing an actual descent. Farmers' boys who have often seen cows and horses lie down and rise, are seldom sure whether the animals rise with their fore or hind feet first, or whether the habit of the horse agrees with that of the cow in this respect. The elm tree has about its leaf a peculiarity which all ought to notice the first time they see it, and yet only about five per cent of a certain school could incorporate in a drawing this peculiarity, although it is so easily outlined on paper. Perception, to achieve satisfactory results, must summon the will to its aid to concentrate the attention. Only the smallest part of what falls upon our senses at any time is actually perceived."

The way to train the mind to receive clear sight-impressions, and therefore to retain them in the memory is simply to concentrate the will and attention upon objects of sight, endeavoring to *see* them plainly and distinctly, and then to practice recalling the details of the object some time afterward. It is astonishing how rapidly one may improve in this respect by a little practice. And it is amazing how great a degree of proficiency in this practice one may attain in a short time. You have doubtless heard the old story of Houdin, the French conjurer, who cultivated his memory of sight impressions by following a simple plan. He started in to practice by observing the number of small objects in the Paris shop windows he could see and remember in one quick glance as he rapidly walked past the window. He followed the plan of noting down on paper the things that he saw and remembered. At first he could remember but two or three articles in the window. Then he began to see and remember more, and so on, each day adding to his power of perception and memory, until finally he was able to see and remember nearly every small article in a large shop window, after bestowing but one glance upon it. Others have found this plan an excellent one, and have developed their power of perception greatly, and at the same time cultivated an amazingly retentive memory of objects thus seen. It is all a matter of use and practice. The experiment of Houdin may be varied infinitely, with excellent results.

The Hindus train their children along these lines, by playing the "sight game" with them. This game is played by exposing to the sight of the children a number of small objects, at which they gaze intently, and which are then withdrawn from their sight. The children then endeavor to excel each other in writing down the names of the objects which they have seen. The number of objects is small to begin with, but is increased each day, until an astonishing number are perceived and remembered.

Rudyard Kipling in his great book, "Kim," gives an instance of this game, played by "Kim" and a trained native youth. Lurgan Sahib exposes to the sight of the two boys a tray filled with jewels and gems, allowing them to gaze upon it a few moments before it is withdrawn from sight. Then the competition begins, as follows: "'There are under that paper five blue stones, one big, one smaller, and three small,' said Kim in all haste. There are four green stones, and one with a hole in it; there is one yellow stone that I can see through, and one like a pipe stem. There are two red stones, and—and—give me time.'"

But Kim had reached the limit of his powers. Then came the turn of the native boy. "'Hear my count,' cried the native child. 'First are two flawed sapphires, one of two ruttes and one of four, as I should judge. The four rutte sapphire is chipped at the edge. There is one Turkestan turquoise, plain with green veins, and there are two inscribed—one with the name of God in gilt, and the other being cracked across, for it came out of an old ring, I cannot read. We have now the five blue stones; four flamed emeralds there are, but one is drilled in two places, and one is a little carven.' 'Their weight?' said Lurgan Sahib, impassively. 'Three—five—five and four ruttees, as I judge it. There is one piece of old greenish amber, and a cheap cut topaz from Europe. There is one ruby of Burma, one of two ruttees, without a flaw. And there is a ballas ruby, flawed, of two ruttees. There is a carved ivory from China, representing a rat sucking an egg; and there is last—Ah—ha!—a ball of crystal as big as a bean set in gold leaf.'" Kim is mortified at his bad beating, and asks the secret. The answer is: "By doing it many times over, till it is done perfectly, for it is worth doing."

Many teachers have followed plans similar to that just related. A number of small articles are exposed, and the pupils are trained to see and remember them, the process being gradually made more and more difficult. A well known American teacher was in the habit of rapidly making a number of dots on the blackboard, and then erasing them before the pupils could count them in the ordinary way. The children then endeavored to count their mental impressions, and before long they could correctly name the number up to ten or more, with ease. They said they could "see six," or "see ten," as the case may be, automatically and apparently without the labour of consciously counting them. It is related in works dealing with the detection of crime, that in the celebrated "thieves schools" in Europe, the young thieves are trained in a similar way, the old scoundrels acting as teachers exposing a number of small articles to the young ones, and requiring them to repeat exactly what they had seen. Then follows a higher course in which the young thieves are required to memorize the objects in a room; the plan of houses, etc. They are sent forth to "spy out the land" for future robberies, in the guise of beggars soliciting alms, and thus getting a rapid peep into houses, offices, and stores. It is said that in a single glance they will perceive the location of all of the doors, windows, locks, bolts, etc.

Many nations have boys' games in which the youngsters are required to see and remember after taking a peep. The Italians have a game called "Morro" in which one boy throws out a number of fingers, which must be instantly named by the other boy, a failure resulting in a forfeit. The Chinese youths have a similar game, while the Japanese boys reduce this to a science. A well trained Japanese youth will be able to remember the entire contents of a room after one keen glance around it. Many of the Orientals have developed this faculty to a degree almost beyond belief. But the principle is the same in all cases—the gradual practice and exercise, beginning with a small number of simple things, and then increasing the number and complexity of the objects.

The faculty is not so rare as one might imagine at first thought. Take a man in a small business, and let him enter the store of a competitor, and see how many things he will observe and remember after a few minutes in the place. Let an actor visit a play in another theatre, and see how many details of the performance he will notice and remember. Let some women pay a visit to a new neighbor, and then see how many things about that house they will have seen and remembered to be retailed to their confidential friends afterward. It is the old story of attention following the interest, and memory following the attention. An expert whist player will see and remember every card played in the game, and just who played it. A chess or checker player will see and remember the previous moves in the game, if he be expert, and can relate them afterward. A woman will go shopping and will see and remember thousands of things that a man would never have seen, much less remembered. As Houdin said: "Thus, for instance, I can safely assert that a lady seeing another pass at full speed in a carriage will have had time to analyze her toilette from her bonnet to her shoes, and be able to describe not only the fashion and quality of the stuffs, but also say if the lace be real or only machine made. I have known ladies to do this."

But, remember this—for it is important: Whatever can be done in this direction by means of attention, inspired by interest, may be duplicated by *attention directed by will.* In other words, the desire to accomplish the task adds and creates an artificial interest just as effective as the natural feeling. And, as you progress, the interest in the game-task will add new interest, and you will be able to duplicate any of the feats mentioned above. It is all a matter of attention, interest (natural or induced) and practice. Begin with a set of dominoes, if you like, and try to remember the spots on one of them rapidly glanced at—then two—then three. By increasing the number gradually, you will attain a power of perception and a memory of sight-impressions that will appear almost marvellous. And not only will you begin to remember dominoes, but you will also be able to perceive and remember thousands of little details of interest, in everything, that have heretofore escaped your notice. The principle is very simple, but the results that may be obtained by practice are wonderful.

The trouble with most of you is that you have been looking without seeing—gazing but not observing. The objects around you have been out of your mental focus. If you will but change your mental focus, by means of will and attention, you will be able to cure yourself of the careless methods of seeing and observing that have been hindrances to your success. You have been blaming it on your memory, but the fault is with your perception. How can the memory remember, when it is not given anything in the way of clear impressions? You have been like young infants in this matter—now it is time for you to begin to "sit up and take notice," no matter how old you may be. The whole thing in a nut-shell is this: In order to remember the things that pass before your sight, you must begin to *see with your mind*, instead of with your retina. Let the impression get beyond your retina and into your mind. If you will do this, you will find that memory will "do the rest."

Chapter 10

Training the Ear

The sense of hearing is one of the highest of the senses or channels whereby we receive impressions from the outside world. In fact, it ranks almost as high as the sense of sight. In the senses of taste, touch, and smell there is a direct contact between the sensitive recipient nerve substance and the particles of the object sensed, while in the sense of sight and the sense of hearing the impression is received through the medium of waves in the ether (in the case of sight), or waves in the air (in the sense of hearing.) Moreover in taste, smell and touch the objects sensed are brought into direct contact with the terminal nerve apparatus, while in seeing and hearing the nerves terminate in peculiar and delicate sacs which contain a fluidic substance through which the impression is conveyed to the nerve proper. Loss of this fluidic substance destroys the faculty to receive impressions, and deafness or blindness ensues. As Foster says: "Waves of sound falling upon the auditory nerve itself produces no effect whatever; it is only when, by the medium of the endolymph, they are brought to bear on the delicate and peculiar epithelium cells which constitute the peripheral terminations of the nerve, that sensations of sound arise."

Just as it is true that it is the mind and not the eye that really *sees*; so is it true that it is the mind and not the ear that really *hears*. Many sounds reach the ear that are not registered by the mind. We pass along a crowded street, the waves of many sounds reaching the nerves of the ear, and yet the mind *accepts* the sounds of but few things, particularly when the novelty of the sounds has passed away. It is a matter of interest and attention in this case, as well as in the case of hearing. As Halleck says: "If we sit by an open window in the country on a summer day, we may have many stimuli knocking at the gate of attention: the ticking of a clock, the sound of the wind, the cackling of fowl, the quacking of ducks, the barking of dogs, the lowing of cows, the cries of children at play, the rustling of leaves, the songs of birds, the rumbling of wagons, etc. If attention is centered upon any one of these, that for the time being acquires the importance of a king upon the throne of our mental world."

Many persons complain of not being able to remember sounds, or things reaching the mind through the sense of hearing, and attribute the trouble to some defect in the organs of hearing. But in so doing they overlook the real cause of the trouble, for it is a scientific fact that many of such persons are found to have hearing apparatus perfectly developed and in the best working order—their trouble arising from a lack of training of the mental faculty of hearing. In other words the trouble is in their mind instead of in the organs of hearing. To acquire the faculty of correct hearing, and correct memory of things heard, the mental faculty of hearing must be exercised, trained and developed. Given a number of people whose hearing apparatus are equally perfect, we will find that some "hear" much better than others; and some hear certain things better than they do certain other things; and that there is a great difference in the grades and degrees of memory of the things heard. As Kay says: "Great differences exist among individuals with regard to the acuteness of this sense (hearing) and some possess it in greater perfection in certain directions than in others. One whose hearing is good for sound in general may yet have but little ear for musical tones; and, on the other hand, one with a good year for music may yet be deficient as regards hearing in general." The secret of this is to be found in the degree of interest and attention bestowed upon the particular thing giving forth the sound.

It is a fact that the mind will hear the faintest sounds from things in which is centered interest and attention, while at the same time ignoring things in which there is no interest and to which the attention is not turned. A sleeping mother will awaken at the slightest whimper from her babe, while the rumbling of a heavy wagon on the street, or even the discharge of a gun in the neighborhood may not be noticed by her. An engineer will detect the slightest difference in the whir or hum of his engine, while failing to notice a very loud noise outside. A musician will note the slightest discord occurring in a concert in which there are a great number of instruments being played, and in which there is a great volume of sound reaching the ear, while other sounds may be unheard by him. The man who taps the wheels of your railroad car is able to detect the slightest difference in tone, and is thus informed that there is a crack or flaw in the wheel. One who handles large quantities of coin will have his attention drawn to the slightest difference in the "ring" of a piece of gold or silver, that informs him that there is something wrong with the coin. A train engineer will distinguish the strange whir of something wrong with the train behind him, amidst all the thundering rattle and roar in which it is merged. The foreman in a machine shop in the same manner detects the little strange noise that informs him that something is amiss, and he rings off the power at once. Telegraphers are able to detect the almost imperceptible differences in the sound of their instruments that inform them that a new operator is on the wire; or just who is sending the message; and, in some cases, the mood or temper of the person transmitting it. Trainmen and steamboat men recognize the differences between every engine or boat on their line, or river, as the case may be. A skilled physician will detect the faint sounds denoting a respiratory trouble or a "heart murmur" in the patients. And yet these very people who are able to detect the faint differences in sound, above mentioned, are often known as "poor hearers" in other things. Why? Simply because they hear only that in which they are interested, and to which their attention has been directed. That is the whole secret, and in it is also to be found the secret of training of the ear-perception. It is all a matter of interest and attention—the details depend upon these principles.

In view of the facts just stated, it will be seen that the remedy for "poor hearing," and poor memory of things heard is to be found in the use of the will in the direction of voluntary attention and interest. So true is this that some authorities go so far as to claim that many cases of supposed slight deafness are really but the result of lack of attention and concentration on the part of the person so troubled. Kay says: "What is commonly called deafness is not infrequently to be attributed to this cause—the sounds being heard but not being interpreted or recognized...

sounds may be distinctly heard when the attention is directed toward them, that in ordinary circumstances would be imperceptible; and people often fail to hear what is said to them because they are not paying attention." Harvey says: "That one-half of the deafness that exists is the result of inattention cannot be doubted." There are but few persons who have not had the experience of listening to some bore, whose words were distinctly heard but the meaning of which was entirely lost because of inattention and lack of interest. Kirkes sums the matter up in these words: "In hearing we must distinguish two different points—the audible sensation as it is developed without any intellectual interference, and the conception which we form in consequence of that sensation."

The reason that many persons do not remember things that they have heard is simply because they have not *listened* properly. Poor listening is far more common than one would suppose at first. A little self-examination will reveal to you the fact that you have fallen into the bad habit of inattention. One cannot listen to everything, of course—it would not be advisable. But one should acquire the habit of either really listening or else refusing to listen at all. The compromise of careless listening brings about deplorable results, and is really the reason why so many people "can't remember" what they have heard. It is all a matter of habit. Persons who have poor memories of ear-impressions should begin to "listen" in earnest. In order to reacquire their lost habit of proper listening, they must exercise voluntary attention and develop interest. The following suggestions may be useful in that direction.

Try to memorize words that are spoken to you in conversation—a few sentences, or even one, at a time. You will find that the effort made to fasten the sentence on your memory will result in a concentration of the attention on the words of the speaker. Do the same thing when you are listening to a preacher, actor or lecturer. Pick out the first sentence for memorizing, and make up your mind that your memory will be as wax to receive the impression and as steel to retain it. Listen to the stray scraps of conversation that come to your ears while walking on the street, and endeavor to memorize a sentence or two, as if you were to repeat it later in the day. Study the various tones, expressions and inflections in the voices of persons speaking to you—you will find this most interesting and helpful. You will be surprised at the details that such analysis will reveal. Listen to the footsteps of different persons and endeavor to distinguish between them—each has its peculiarities. Get someone to read a line or two of poetry or prose to you, and then endeavor to remember it. A little practice of this kind will greatly develop the power of voluntary attention to sounds and spoken words. But above everything else, practice repeating the words and sounds that you have memorized, so far as is possible—for by so doing you will get the mind into the habit of taking an interest in sound impressions. In this way you not only improve the sense of hearing, but also the faculty of remembering.

If you will analyze, and boil down the above remarks and directions, you will find that the gist of the whole matter is that one should *actually use, employ and exercise* the mental faculty of hearing, actively and intelligently. Nature has a way of putting to sleep, or atrophying any faculty that is not used or exercised; and also of encouraging, developing and strengthening any faculty that is properly employed and exercised. In this you have the secret. Use it. If you will listen well, you will hear well and remember well that which you have heard.

Chapter 11

How to Remember Names

The phase of memory connected with the remembrance or recollection of names probably is of greater interest to the majority of persons than are any of the associated phases of the subject. On all hands are to be found people who are embarassed by their failure to recall the name of someone whom they feel they know, but whose name has escaped them. This failure to remember the names of persons undoubtedly interferes with the business and professional success of many persons; and, on the other hand, the ability to recall names readily has aided many persons in the struggle for success. It would seem that there are a greater number of persons deficient in this phase of memory than in any other. As Holbrook has said: "The memory of names is a subject with which most persons must have a more than passing interest... The number of persons who never or rarely forget a name is exceedingly small, the number of those who have a poor memory for them is very large. The reason for this is partly a defect of mental development and partly a matter of habit. In either case it may be overcome by effort... I have satisfied myself by experience and observation that a memory for names may be increased not only two, *but a hundredfold.*"

You will find that the majority of successful men have been able to recall the faces and names of those with whom they came in contact, and it is an interesting subject for speculation as to just how much of their success was due to this faculty. Socrates is said to have easily remembered the names of all of his students, and his classes numbered thousands in the course of a year. Xenophon is said to have known the name of every one of his soldiers, which faculty was shared by Washington and Napoleon, also. Trajan is said to have known the names of all the Praetorian Guards, numbering about 12,000. Pericles knew the face and name of every one of the citizens of Athens. Cineas is said to have known the names of all the citizens of Rome. Themistocles knew the names of 20,000 Athenians. Lucius Scipio could call by name every citizen of Rome. John Wesley could recall the names of thousands of persons whom he had met in his travels. Henry Clay was specially developed in this phase of memory, and there was a tradition among his followers that he remembered every one whom he met. Blaine had a similar reputation.

There have been many theories advanced, and explanations offered to account for the fact that the recollection of names is far more difficult than any other form of the activities of the memory. We shall not take up your time in going over these theories, but shall proceed upon the theory now generally accepted by the best authorities; i.e. that the difficulty in the recollection of names is caused by the fact that names in themselves are *uninteresting* and therefore do not attract or hold the attention as do other objects presented to the mind. There is of course to be remembered the fact that sound impressions are apt to be more difficult of recollection than sight impressions, but the lack of interesting qualities in names is believed to be the principal obstacle and difficulty. Fuller says of this matter: "A proper noun, or name, when considered independently of accidental features of coincidence with something that is familiar, *doesn't mean anything*; for this reason a mental picture of it is not easily formed, which accounts for the fact that the primitive, tedious way of rote, or repetition, is that ordinarily employed to impress a proper noun on the memory, while a common noun, being represented by some object having shape, or appearance, in the physical or mental perception, can thus be *seen or imagined*: in other words *a mental image* of it can be formed and the *name* identified afterwards, through associating it with this mental image." We think that the case is fully stated in this quotation.

But in spite of this difficulty, persons have and can greatly improve their memory of names. Many who were originally very deficient in this respect have not only improved the faculty far beyond its former condition, but have also developed exceptional ability in this special phase of memory so that they became noted for their unfailing recollection of the names of those with whom they came in contact.

Perhaps the best way to impress upon you the various methods that may be used for this purpose would be to relate to you the actual experience of a gentleman employed in a bank in one of the large cities of this country, who made a close study of the subject and developed himself far beyond the ordinary. Starting with a remarkably poor memory for names, he is now known to his associates as "the man who never forgets a name." This gentleman first took a number of "courses" in secret "methods" of developing the memory; but after thus spending much money he expressed his disgust with the whole idea of artificial memory training. He then started in to study the subject from the point-of-view of The New Psychology, putting into effect all of the tested principles, and improving upon some of their details. We have had a number of conversations with this gentleman, and have found that his experience confirms many of our own ideas and theories, and the fact that he has demonstrated the correctness of the principles to such a remarkable degree renders his case one worthy of being stated in the direction of affording a guide and "method" for others who wish to develop their memory of names.

The gentleman, whom we shall call "Mr. X.," decided that the first thing for him to do was to develop his faculty of receiving clear and distinct sound impressions. In doing this he followed the plan outlined by us in our chapter on "Training the Ear." He persevered and practiced along these lines until his "hearing" became very acute. He made a study of voices, until he could classify them and analyze their characteristics. Then he found that he could *hear* names in a manner before impossible to him. That is, instead of merely catching a vague sound of a name, he would hear it so clearly and distinctly that a firm registration would be obtained on the records of his memory. For the first time in his life names began to *mean something* to him. He paid attention to every name he heard, just as he did to every note he handled. He would repeat a name to himself, after hearing it, and would thus strengthen the impression. If he came across an unusual name, he would write it down several times, at the first opportunity, thus obtaining the benefit of a double sense impression, adding eye impression to ear impression.

All this, of course, aroused his interest in the subject of names in general, which led him to the next step in his progress.

Mr. X. then began to study names, their origin, their peculiarities, their differences, points of resemblances, etc. He made a hobby of names, and evinced all the joy of a collector when he was able to stick the pin of attention through the specimen of a new and unfamiliar species of name. He began to collect names, just as others collect beetles, stamps, coins, etc., and took quite a pride in his collection and in his knowledge of the subject. He read books on names, from the libraries, giving their origin, etc. He had the Dickens' delight in "queer" names, and would amuse his friends by relating the funny names he had seen on signs, and otherwise. He took a small City Directory home with him, and would run over the pages in the evening, looking up new names, and classifying old ones into groups. He found that some names were derived from animals, and put these into a class by themselves—the Lyons, Wolfs, Foxes, Lambs, Hares, etc. Others were put into the color group—Blacks, Greens, Whites, Greys, Blues, etc. Others belonged to the bird family—Crows, Hawks, Birds, Drakes, Cranes, Doves, Jays, etc. Others belonged to trades—Millers, Smiths, Coopers, Maltsters, Carpenters, Bakers, Painters, etc. Others were trees—Chestnuts, Oakleys, Walnuts, Cherrys, Pines, etc. Then there were Hills and Dales; Fields and Mountains; Lanes and Brooks. Some were Strong; others were Gay; others were Savage; others Noble. And so on. It would take a whole book to tell you what that man found out about names. He came near becoming a "crank" on the subject. But his hobby began to manifest excellent results, for his *interest* had been awakened to an unusual degree, and he was becoming very proficient in his recollection of names, for they now meant something to him.

He easily recalled all the regular customers at his bank,—quite a number by the way for the bank was a large one—and many occasional depositors were delighted to have themselves called by name by our friend. Occasionally he would meet with a name that balked him, in which case he would repeat it over to himself, and write it a number of times until he had mastered it—after that it never escaped him.

Mr. X. would always repeat a name when it was spoken, and would at the same time look intently at the person bearing it, thus seeming to fix the two together in his mind at the same time—when he wanted them they would be found in each other's company. He also acquired the habit of *visualizing* the name—that is, he would see its letters in his mind's eye, as a picture. This he regarded as a most important point, and we thoroughly agree with him. He used the Law of Association in the direction of associating a new man with a well-remembered man of the same name. A new Mr. Schmidtzenberger would be associated with an old customer of the same name—when he would see the new man, he would think of the old one, and the name would flash into his mind. To sum up the whole method, however, it may be said that the gist of the thing was in *taking an interest* in names in general. In this way an uninteresting subject was made interesting—and a man always has a good memory for the things in which he is interested.

The case of Mr. X. is an extreme one—and the results obtained were beyond the ordinary. But if you will take a leaf from his book, you may obtain the same results in the degree that you work for it. Make a study of names—start a collection—and you will have no trouble in developing a memory for them. This is the whole thing in a nut-shell.

Chapter 12

How to Remember Faces

The memory of faces is closely connected with the memory of names, and yet the two are not always associated, for there are many people who easily remember faces, and yet forget names, and vice versa. In some ways, however, the memory of faces is a necessary precedent for the recollection of the names of people. For unless we recall the face, we are unable to make the necessary association with the name of the person. We have given a number of instances of face-memory, in our chapter on name-memory, in which are given instances of the wonderful memory of celebrated individuals who acquired a knowledge and memory of the thousands of citizens of a town, or city, or the soldiers of an army. In this chapter, however, we shall pay attention only to the subject of the recollection of the features of persons, irrespective of their names. This faculty is possessed by all persons, but in varying degrees. Those in whom it is well developed seem to recognize the faces of persons whom they have met years before, and to associate them with the circumstances in which they last met them, even where the name escapes the memory. Others seem to forget a face the moment it passes from view, and fail to recognize the same persons whom they met only a few hours before, much to their mortification and chagrin.

Detectives, newspaper reporters, and others who come in contact with many people, usually have this faculty largely developed, for it becomes a necessity of their work, and their interest and attention is rendered active thereby. Public men often have this faculty largely developed by reason of the necessities of their life. It is said that James G. Blaine never forgot the face of anyone whom he had met and conversed with a few moments. This faculty rendered him very popular in political life. In this respect he resembled Henry Clay, who was noted for his memory of faces. It is related of Clay that he once paid a visit of a few hours to a small town in Mississippi, on an electioneering tour. Amidst the throng surrounding him was an old man, with one eye missing. The old fellow pressed forward crying out that he was sure that Henry Clay would remember him. Clay took a sharp look at him and said: "I met you in Kentucky many years ago, did I not?" "Yes," replied the man. "Did you lose your eye since then?" asked Clay. "Yes, several years after," replied the old man. "Turn your face side-ways, so that I can see your profile," said Clay. The man did so. Then Clay smiled, triumphantly, saying: "I've got you now—weren't you on that jury in the Innes case at Frankfort, that I tried in the United States Court over twenty years ago?" "Yes siree!" said the man, "I knowed that ye know me, 'n I told 'em you would." And the crowd gave a whoop, and Clay knew that he was safe in that town and county.

Vidocq, the celebrated French detective, is said to have never forgotten a face of a criminal whom he had once seen.

A celebrated instance of this power on his part is that of the case of Delafranche the forger who escaped from prison and dwelt in foreign lands for over twenty years. After that time here turned to Paris feeling secure from detection, having become bald, losing an eye, and having his nose badly mutilated. Moreover he disguised himself and wore a beard, in order to still further evade detection. One day Vidocq met him on the street, and recognized him at once, his arrest and return to prison following. Instances of this kind could be multiplied indefinitely, but the student will have had a sufficient acquaintance with persons who possess this faculty developed to a large degree, so that further illustration is scarcely necessary.

The way to develop this phase of memory is akin to that urged in the development of other phases—the cultivation of interest, and the bestowal of attention. Faces as a whole are not apt to prove interesting. It is only by analyzing and classifying them that the study begins to grow of interest to us. The study of a good elementary work on physiognomy is recommended to those wishing to develop the faculty of remembering faces, for in such a work the student is led to notice the different kinds of noses, ears, eyes, chins, foreheads, etc., such notice and recognition tending to induce an interest in the subject of features. A rudimentary course of study in drawing faces, particularly in profile, will also tend to make one "take notice" and will awaken interest. If you are required to draw a nose, particularly from memory, you will be apt to give to it your interested attention. The matter of interest is vital. If you were shown a man and told that the next time you met and recognized him he would hand you over $500, you would be very apt to study his face carefully, and to recognize him later on; whereas the same man if introduced casually as a "Mr. Jones," would arouse no interest and the chances of recognition would be slim.

Halleck says: "Every time we enter a street car we see different types of people, and there is a great deal to be noticed about each type. Every human countenance shows its past history to one who knows how to look... Successful gamblers often become so expert in noticing the slightest change of an opponent's facial expression that they will estimate the strength of his hand by the involuntary signs which appear in the face and which are frequently checked the instant they appear."

Of all classes, perhaps artists are more apt to form a clear cut image of the features of persons whom they meet—particularly if they are portrait painters. There are instances of celebrated portrait painters who were able to execute a good portrait after having once carefully studied the face of the sitter, their memory enabling them to visualize the features at will. Some celebrated teachers of drawing have instructed their scholars to take a sharp hasty glance at a nose, an eye, an ear, or chin, and then to so clearly visualize it that they could draw it perfectly. It is all a matter of interest, attention, *and practice.* Sir Francis Galton cites the instance of a French teacher who trained his pupils so thoroughly in this direction that after a few months' practice they had no difficulty in summoning images at will; in holding them steady; and in drawing them correctly. He says of the faculty of visualization thus used: "A faculty that is of importance in all technical and artistic occupations, that gives accuracy to our perceptions, and justice to our generalizations, is starved by lazy disuse, instead of being cultivated judiciously in such a way as will, on the whole, bring the best return. I believe that a serious study of the best means of developing and utilizing this faculty, without prejudice to the practice of abstract thought in symbols, is one of the many pressing desiderata in the yet unformed science of education."

Fuller relates the method of a celebrated painter, which method has been since taught by many teachers of both drawing and memory. He relates it as follows: "The celebrated painter Leonardo da Vinci invented a most ingenious method for identifying faces, and by it is said to have been able to reproduce from memory any face that he had once carefully scrutinized. He drew all the possible forms of the nose, mouth, chin, eyes, ears and forehead, numbered them 1, 2, 3, 4, etc., and committed them thoroughly to memory; then, whenever he saw a face that he wished to draw or paint from memory, he noted in his mind that it was chin 4, eyes 2, nose 5, ears 6,—or whatever the combinations might be—and by retaining the analysis in his memory he could reconstruct the face at any time." We could scarcely ask the student to attempt so complicated a system, and yet a modification of it would prove useful. That is, if you would begin to form a classification of several kind of noses, say about seven, the well-known Roman, Jewish, Grecian, giving you the general classes, in connection with straight, crooked, pug and all the other varieties, you would soon recognize noses when you saw them. And the same with mouths, a few classes being found to cover the majority of cases. But of all the features, the eye is the most expressive, and the one most easily remembered, when clearly noticed. Detectives rely much upon *the expression of the eye*. If you ever fully catch the *expression* of a person's eye, you will be very apt to recognize it thereafter. Therefore concentrate on eyes in studying faces.

A good plan in developing this faculty is to visualize the faces of persons you have met during the day, in the evening. Try to develop the faculty of visualizing the features of those whom you know—this will start you off right. Draw them in your mind—see them with your mind's eye, until you can visualize the features of very old friends; then do the same with acquaintances, and so on, until you are able to visualize the features of every one you "know." Then start on to add to your list by recalling in the imagination, the features of strangers whom you meet. By a little practice of this kind you will develop a great interest in faces and your memory of them, and the power to recall them will increase rapidly. The secret is to study faces—to be interested in them. In this way you add zest to the task, and make a pleasure of a drudgery. The study of photographs is also a great aid in this work—but study them in detail, not as a whole. If you can arouse sufficient interest in features and faces, you will have no trouble in remembering and recalling them. The two things go together.

Chapter 13

How to Remember Places

There is a great difference in the various degrees of development of "the sense of locality" in different persons. But these differences may be traced directly to the degree of memory of that particular phase or faculty of the mind, which in turn depends upon the degree of attention, interest, and use which has been bestowed upon the faculty in question. The authorities on phrenology define the faculty of "locality" as follows: "Cognizance of place; recollection of the looks of places, roads, scenery, and the location of objects; where on a page ideas are to be found, and position generally; the geographical faculty; the desire to see places, and have the ability to find them." Persons in whom this faculty is developed to the highest degree seem to have an almost intuitive idea of direction, place and position. They never get lost or "mixed up" regarding direction or place. They remember the places they visit and their relation in space to each other. Their minds are like maps upon which are engraved the various roads, streets and objects of sight in every direction. When these people think of China, Labrador, Terra del Fuego,

Norway, Cape of Good Hope, Thibet, or any other place, they seem to think of it in "*this* direction or *that* direction" rather than as a vague place situated in a vague direction. Their minds think "north, south, east or west" as the case may be when they consider a given place. Shading down by degrees we find people at the other pole of the faculty who seem to find it impossible to remember any direction, or locality or relation in space. Such people are constantly losing themselves in their own towns, and fear to trust themselves in a strange place. They have no sense of direction, or place, and fail to recognize a street or scene which they have visited recently, not to speak of those which they travelled over in time past. Between these two poles or degrees there is a vast difference, and it is difficult to realize that it is all a matter of use, interest and attention. That it is but this may be proven by anyone who will take the trouble and pains to develop the faculty and memory of locality within his mind. Many have done this, and anyone else may do likewise if the proper methods be employed.

The secret of the development of the faculty and memory of place and locality is akin to that mentioned in the preceding chapter, in connection with the development of the memory for names. The first thing necessary is to develop an *interest* in the subject. One should begin to "take notice" of the direction of the streets or roads over which he travels; the landmarks; the turns of the road; the natural objects along the way. He should study maps, until he awakens a new interest in them, just as did the man who used the directory in order to take an interest in names. He should procure a small geography and study direction, distances, location, shape and form of countries, etc., not as a mere mechanical thing but as a live subject of interest. If there were a large sum of money awaiting your coming in certain sections of the globe, you would manifest a decided interest in the direction, locality and position of those places, and the best way to reach them. Before long you would be a veritable reference book regarding those special places. Or, if your sweetheart were waiting for you in some such place, you would do likewise. The whole thing lies in the degree of "want to" regarding the matter. Desire awakens interest; interest employs attention; and attention brings use, development and memory. Therefore you must first *want to* develop the faculty of Locality—and want to "hard enough." The rest is a mere matter of detail.

One of the first things to do, after arousing an interest, is to carefully note the landmarks and relative positions of the streets or roads over which you travel. So many people travel along a new street or road in an absent-minded manner, taking no notice of the lay of the land as they proceed. This is fatal to place-memory. You must take notice of the thoroughfares and the things along the way. Pause at the cross roads, or the street-corners and note the landmarks, and the general directions and relative positions, until they are firmly imprinted on your mind. Begin to see how many things you can remember regarding even a little exercise walk. And when you have returned home, go over the trip in your mind, and see how much of the direction and how many of the landmarks you are able to remember. Take out your pencil, and endeavor to *make a map* of your route, giving the general directions, and noting the street names, and principal objects of interest. Fix the idea of "North" in your mind when starting, and keep your bearings by it during your whole trip, and in your map making. You will be surprised how much interest you will soon develop in this map-making. It will get to be quite a game, and you will experience pleasure in your increasing proficiency in it. When you go out for a walk, go in a round-about way, taking as many turns and twists as possible, in order to exercise your faculty of locality and direction—but always note carefully direction and general course, so that you may reproduce it correctly on your map when you return. If you have a city map, compare it with your own little map, and also re-trace your route, in imagination, on the map. With a city map, or road-map, you may get lots of amusement by re-travelling the route of your little journeys.

Always note the names of the various streets over which you travel, as well as those which you cross during your walk. Note them down upon your map, and you will find that you will develop a rapidly improving memory in this direction—because you have awakened interest and bestowed attention. Take a pride in your map making. If you have a companion, endeavor to beat each other at this game—both travelling over the same route together, and then seeing which one can remember the greatest number of details of the journey.

Akin to this, and supplementary to it, is the plan of selecting a route to be travelled, on your city map, endeavoring to fix in your mind the general directions, names of streets, turns, return journey, etc., before you start. Begin by mapping out a short trip in this way, and then increase it every day. After mapping out a trip, lay aside your map and travel it in person. If you like, take along the map and puzzle out variations, from time to time. Get the map habit in every possible variation and form, but do not depend upon the map exclusively; but instead, endeavor to correlate the printed map with the mental map that you are building in your brain.

If you are about to take a journey to a strange place, study your maps carefully before you go, and exercise your memory in reproducing them with a pencil. Then as you travel along, compare places with your map, and you will find that you will take an entirely new interest in the trip—it will begin by meaning something to you. If about to visit a strange city, procure a map of it before starting, and begin by noting the cardinal points of the compass, study the map—the directions of the principal streets and the relative positions of the principal points of interest, buildings, etc. In this way you not only develop your memory of places, and render yourself proof against being lost, but you also provide a source of new and great interest in your visit.

The above suggestions are capable of the greatest expansion and variation on the part of anyone who practices them. The whole thing depends upon the "taking notice" and using the attention, and those things in turn depend upon the taking of interest in the subject. If anyone will "wake up and take interest" in the subject of locality and direction he may develop himself along the lines of place-memory to an almost incredible degree, in a comparatively short time at that. There is no other phase of memory that so quickly responds to use and exercise as this one. We have in mind a lady who was notoriously deficient in the memory of place, and was sure to lose herself a few blocks from her stopping place, wherever she might be. She seemed absolutely devoid of the sense of direction or locality and often lost herself in the hotel corridors, notwithstanding the fact that she travelled all over the world, with her husband, for years. The trouble undoubtedly arose from the fact that she depended altogether upon her husband as a pilot, the couple being inseparable. Well, the husband died, and the lady lost her pilot. Instead of giving up in despair, she began to rise to the occasion—having no pilot, she had to pilot herself. And she was forced to "wake up and take notice." She was compelled to travel for a couple of years, in order to close up certain business matters of her husband's—for she was a good business woman in spite of her lack of development along this one line—and in order to get around safely, she was forced to take an interest in where she was going. Before the two years' travels were over, she was as good a traveller as her husband had ever been, and was frequently called upon as a guide by others in whose company she chanced to be. She explained it by saying "Why, I don't know just how I did it—I just *had to*, that's all—I just *did* it." Another example of a woman's "because," you see. What this good lady "just did," was accomplished by an instinctive following of the plan which we have suggested to you. She "just *had* to" use maps and to "take notice." That is the whole story.

So true are the principles underlying this method of developing the place-memory, that one deficient in it, providing he will arouse intense interest and will stick to it, may develop the faculty to such an extent that he may almost rival the cat which "always came back," or the dog which "you couldn't lose." The Indians, Arabs, Gypsies and other people of the plain, forest, desert, and mountains, have this faculty so highly developed that it seems almost like an extra sense. It is all this matter of "taking notice" sharpened by continuous need, use and exercise, to a high degree. The mind will respond to the need if the person like the lady, "just *has to*." The laws of Attention and Association will work wonders when actively called into play by Interest or need, followed by exercise and use. There is no magic in the process—just "want to" and "keep at it," that's all. Do you want to hard enough—have you the determination to keep at it?

Chapter 14

How to Remember Numbers

The faculty of Number—that is the faculty of knowing, recognizing and remembering figures in the abstract and in their relation to each other, differs very materially among different individuals. To some, figures and numbers are apprehended and remembered with ease, while to others they possess no interest, attraction or affinity, and consequently are not apt to be remembered. It is generally admitted by the best authorities that the memorizing of dates, figures, numbers, etc., is the most difficult of any of the phases of memory. But all agree that the faculty may be developed by practice and interest. There have been instances of persons having this faculty of the mind developed to a degree almost incredible; and other instances of persons having started with an aversion to figures and then developing an interest which resulted in their acquiring a remarkable degree of proficiency along these lines.

Many of the celebrated mathematicians and astronomers developed wonderful memories for figures. Herschel is said to have been able to remember all the details of intricate calculations in his astronomical computations, even to the figures of the fractions. It is said that he was able to perform the most intricate calculations mentally, without the use of pen or pencil, and then dictated to his assistant the entire details of the process, including the final results. Tycho Brahe, the astronomer, also possessed a similar memory. It is said that he rebelled at being compelled to refer to the printed tables of square roots and cube roots, and set to work to memorize the entire set of tables, which almost incredible task he accomplished in a half day—this required the memorizing of over 75,000 figures, and their relations to each other. Euler the mathematician became blind in his old age, and being unable to refer to his tables, memorized them. It is said that he was able to repeat from recollection the first six powers of all the numbers from one to one hundred.

Wallis the mathematician was a prodigy in this respect. He is reported to have been able to mentally extract the square root of a number to forty decimal places, and on one occasion mentally extracted the cube root of a number consisting of thirty figures. Dase is said to have mentally multiplied two numbers of one hundred figures each. A youth named Mangiamele was able to perform the most remarkable feats in mental arithmetic. The reports show that upon a celebrated test before members of the French Academy of Sciences he was able to extract the cube root of 3,796,416 in thirty seconds; and the tenth root of 282,475,289 in three minutes. He also immediately solved the following question put to him by Arago: "What number has the following proportion: That if five times the number be subtracted from the cube plus five times the square of the number, and nine times the square of the number be subtracted from that result, the remainder will be 0?" The answer, "5" was given immediately, without putting down a figure on paper or board. It is related that a cashier of a Chicago bank was able to mentally restore the accounts of the bank, which had been destroyed in the great fire in that city, and his account which was accepted by the bank and the depositors, was found to agree perfectly with the other memoranda in the case, the work performed by him being solely the work of his memory.

Bidder was able to tell instantly the number of farthings in the sum of £868, 42s, 121d. Buxton mentally calculated the number of cubical eighths of an inch there were in a quadrangular mass 23,145,789 yards long, 2,642,732 yards wide and 54,965 yards in thickness. He also figured out mentally, the dimensions of an irregular estate of about a thousand acres, giving the contents in acres and perches, then reducing them to square inches, and then reducing them to square hair-breadths, estimating 2,304 to the square inch, 48 to each side. The mathematical prodigy, Zerah Colburn, was perhaps the most remarkable of any of these remarkable people. When a mere child, he began to develop the most amazing qualities of mind regarding figures. He was able to instantly make the mental calculation of the exact number of seconds or minutes there was in a given time. On one occasion he calculated the number of minutes and seconds contained in forty-eight years, the answer: "25,228,800 minutes, and 1,513,728,000 seconds," being given almost instantaneously. He could instantly multiply any number of one to three figures, by another number consisting of the same number of figures; the factors of any number consisting of six or seven figures; the square, and cube roots, and the prime numbers of any numbers given him. He mentally raised the number 8, progressively, to its sixteenth power, the result being 281,474,976,710,656; and gave the square root of 106,929, which was 5. He mentally extracted the cube root of 268,336,125; and the squares of 244,999,755 and 1,224,998,755. In five seconds he calculated the cube root of 413,993,348,677. He found the factors of 4,294,967,297, which had previously been considered to be a prime number. He mentally calculated the square of 999,999, which is 999,998,000,001 and then multiplied that number by 49, and the product by the same number, and the whole by 25—the latter as extra measure.

The great difficulty in remembering numbers, to the majority of persons, is the fact that numbers "do not mean anything to them"—that is, that numbers are thought of only in their abstract phase and nature, and are consequently far more difficult to remember than are impressions received from the senses of sight or sound. The remedy, however, becomes apparent when we recognize the source of the difficulty. The remedy is: *Make the number the subject of sound and sight impressions.* Attach the abstract idea of the numbers to the sense of impressions of sight or sound, or both, according to which are the best developed in your particular case. It may be difficult for you to remember "1848" as an abstract thing, but comparatively easy for you to remember the *sound* of "eighteen forty-eight," or the *shape and appearance* of "1848." If you will repeat a number to yourself, so that you grasp the sound impression of it, or else visualize it so that you can remember having *seen* it—then you will be far more apt to remember it than if you merely think of it without reference to sound or form. You may forget that the number of a certain store or house is 3948, but you may easily remember the sound of the spoken words "thirty-nine forty-eight," or the form of "3948" as it appeared to your sight on the door of the place. In the latter case, you associate the number with the door and when you visualize the door you visualize the number.

Kay, speaking of visualization, or the reproduction of mental images of things to be remembered, says: "Those who have been distinguished for their power to carry out long and intricate processes of mental calculation owe it to the same cause." Taine says: "Children accustomed to calculate in their heads write mentally with chalk on an imaginary board the figures in question, then all their partial operations, then the final sum, so that they see internally the different lines of white figures with which they are concerned. Young Colburn, who had never been at school and did not know how to read or write, said that, when making his calculations 'he saw them clearly before him.' Another said that he 'saw the numbers he was working with as if they had been written on a slate.'" Bidder said: "If I perform a sum mentally, it always proceeds in a visible form in my mind; indeed, I can conceive of no other way possible of doing mental arithmetic."

We have known office boys who could never remember the number of an address until it were distinctly repeated to them several times—then they memorized the *sound* and never forget it. Others forget the sounds, or failed to register them in the mind, but after once seeing the number on the door of an office or store, could repeat it at a moment's notice, saying that they mentally "could see the figures on the door." You will find by a little questioning that the majority of people remember figures or numbers in this way, and that very few can remember them as abstract things. For that matter it is difficult for the majority of persons to even think of a number, abstractly. Try it yourself, and ascertain whether you do not remember the number as either a *sound of words*, or else as the mental image or visualization of the *form of the figures*. And, by the way, whichever it happens to be, sight or sound, that particular kind of remembrance is *your* best way of remembering numbers, and consequently gives you the lines upon which you should proceed to develop this phase of memory.

The law of Association may be used advantageously in memorizing numbers; for instance we know of a person who remembered the number 186,000 (the number of miles per second travelled by light-waves in the ether) by associating it with the number of his father's former place of business, "186." Another remembered his telephone number "1876" by recalling the date of the Declaration of Independence. Another, the number of States in the Union, by associating it with the last two figures of the number of his place of business. But by far the better way to memorize dates, special numbers connected with events, etc., is to visualize the picture of the event with the picture of the date or number, thus combining the two things into a mental picture, the association of which will be preserved when the picture is recalled. Verse of doggerel, such as "In fourteen hundred and ninety-two, Columbus sailed the ocean blue;" or "In eighteen hundred and sixty-one, our country's Civil war begun," etc., have their places and uses. But it is far better to cultivate the "sight or sound" of a number, than to depend upon cumbersome associative methods based on artificial links and pegs.

Finally, as we have said in the preceding chapters, before one can develop a good memory of a subject, he must first cultivate an interest in that subject. Therefore, if you will keep your interest in figures alive by working out a few problems in mathematics, once in a while, you will find that figures will begin to have a new interest for you. A little elementary arithmetic, used with interest, will do more to start you on the road to "How to Remember Numbers" than a dozen text books on the subject. In memory, the three rules are: "Interest, Attention and Exercise"—and the last is the most important, for without it the others fail. You will be surprised to see how many interesting things there are in figures, as you proceed. The task of going over the elementary arithmetic will not be nearly so "dry" as when you were a child. You will uncover all sorts of "queer" things in relation to numbers. Just as a "sample" let us call your attention to a few:

Take the figure "1" and place behind it a number of "naughts," thus: 1,000,000,000,000,—as many "naughts" or ciphers as you wish. Then divide the number by the figure "7." You will find that the result is always this "142,857" then another "142,857," and so on to infinity, if you wish to carry the calculation that far. These six figures will be repeated over and over again. Then multiply this "142,857" by the figure "7," and your product will be *all nines*. Then take any number, and set it down, placing beneath it a reversal of itself and subtract the latter from the former, thus:

$$\begin{array}{r} 117{,}761{,}909 \\ \underline{90{,}916{,}771} \\ 26{,}845{,}138 \end{array}$$

and you will find that the result will always reduce to nine, and is always a multiple of 9. Take any number composed of two or more figures, and subtract from it the added sum of its separate figures, and the result is always a multiple of 9, thus:

$$\begin{array}{rl} & 184 \\ 1+8+4 = & \underline{13} \\ & 171 \div 9 = 19 \end{array}$$

We mention these familiar examples merely to remind you that there is much more of interest in mere figures than many would suppose. If you can arouse your interest in them, then you will be well started on the road to the memorizing of numbers. Let figures and numbers "mean something" to you, and the rest will be merely a matter of detail.

Chapter 15

How to Remember Music

Like all of the other faculties of the mind, that of music or tune is manifested in varying degrees by different individuals. To some music seems to be almost instinctively grasped, while to others it is acquired only by great effort and much labor. To some harmony is natural, and inharmony a matter of repulsion, while others fail to recognize the difference between the two except in extreme cases. Some seem to be the very soul of music, while others have no conception of what the soul of music may be. Then there is manifested the different phases of the knowledge of music. Some play correctly by ear, but are clumsy and inefficient when it comes to playing by note. Others play very correctly in a mechanical manner, but fail to retain the memory of music which they have heard. It is indeed a good musician who combines within himself, or herself, both of the two last mentioned faculties—the ear perception of music and the ability to execute correctly from notes.

There are many cases of record in which extraordinary powers of memory of music have been manifested. Fuller relates the following instances of this particular phase of memory: Carolan, the greatest of Irish bards, once met a noted musician and challenged him to a test of their respective musical abilities. The *defi* was accepted and Carolan's rival played on his violin one of Vivaldi's most difficult concertos. On the conclusion of the performance, Carolan, who had never heard the piece before, took his harp and played the concerto through from beginning to end without making a single error. His rival thereupon yielded the palm, thoroughly satisfied of Carolan's superiority, as well he might be. Beethoven could retain in his memory any musical composition, however complex, that he had listened to, and could reproduce most of it. He could play from memory every one of the compositions in Bach's 'Well Tempered Clavichord,' there being forty-eight preludes and the same number of fugues which in intricacy of movement and difficulty of execution are almost unexampled, as each of these compositions is written in the most abstruse style of counterpoint.

"Mozart, at four years of age, could remember note for note, elaborate solos in concertos which he had heard; he could learn a minuet in half an hour, and even composed short pieces at that early age. At six he was able to compose without the aid of an instrument, and continued to advance rapidly in musical memory and knowledge. When fourteen years old he went to Rome in Holy Week. At the Sistine Chapel was performed each day, Allegri's 'Miserere,' the score of which Mozart wished to obtain, but he learned that no copies were allowed to be made. He listened attentively to the performance, at the conclusion of which he wrote the whole score from memory without an error. Another time, Mozart was engaged to contribute an original composition to be performed by a noted violinist and himself at Vienna before the Emperor Joseph. On arriving at the appointed place Mozart discovered that he had forgotten to bring his part. Nothing dismayed, he placed a blank sheet of paper before him, and played his part through from memory without a mistake. When the opera of 'Don Giovanni' was first performed there was no time to copy the score for the harpsichord, but Mozart was equal to the occasion; he conducted the entire opera and played the harpsichord accompaniment to the songs and choruses without a note before him. There are many well-attested instances of Mendelssohn's remarkable musical memory. He once gave a grand concert in London, at which his Overture to 'Midsummer Night's Dream' was produced. There was only one copy of the full score, which was taken charge of by the organist of St. Paul's Cathedral, who unfortunately left it in a hackney coach—whereupon Mendelssohn wrote out another score from memory, without an error. At another time, when about to direct a public performance of Bach's 'Passion Music,' he found on mounting the conductor's platform that instead of the score of the work to be performed, that of another composition had been brought by mistake. Without hesitation Mendelssohn successfully conducted this com plicated work from memory, automatically turning over leaf after leaf of the score before him as the performance progressed, so that no feeling of uneasiness might enter the minds of the orchestra and singers. Gottschalk, it is said, could play from memory several thousand compositions, including many of the works of Bach. The noted conductor, Vianesi, rarely has the score before him in conducting an opera, knowing every note of many operas from memory."

It will be seen that two phases of memory must enter into the "memory of music"—the memory of tune and the memory of the notes. The memory of tune of course falls into the class of ear-impressions, and what has been said regarding them is also applicable to this case. The memory of notes falls into the classification of eye-impressions, and the rules of this class of memory applies in this case. As to the cultivation of the memory of tune, the principle advice to be given is that the student take an active interest in all that pertains to the sound of music, and also takes every opportunity for listening to good music, and endeavoring to reproduce it in the imagination or memory. Endeavor to enter into the spirit of the music until it becomes a part of yourself. Rest not content with merely hearing it, but lend yourself to a *feeling* of its meaning. The more the music "means to you," the more easily will you remember it. The plan followed by many students, particularly those of vocal music, is to have a few bars of a piece played over to them several times, until they are able to hum it correctly; then a few more are added; and then a few more and so on. Each addition must be reviewed in connection with that which was learned before, so that the chain of association may be kept unbroken. The principle is the same as the child learning his A-B-C—he remembers "B" because it follows "A." By this constant addition of "just a little bit more," accompanied by frequent reviews, long and difficult pieces may be memorized.

The memory of notes may be developed by the method above named—the method of learning a few bars well, and then adding a few more, and frequently reviewing as far as you have learned, forging the links of association as you go along, by frequent practice. The method being entirely that of eye-impression and subject to its rules, you must observe the idea of visualization—that is learning each bar until you can *see* it "in your mind's eye" as you proceed. But in this, as in many other eye-impressions, you will find that you will be greatly aided by your memory of the *sound* of the notes, in addition to their appearance. Try to associate the two as much as possible, so that when you *see* a note, you will *hear* the sound of it, and when you *hear* a note sounded, you will *see* it as it appears on the score. This combining of the impressions of both sight and sound will give you the benefit of the double sense impression, which results in doubling your memory efficiency. In addition to visualizing the notes themselves, the student should add the appearance of the various symbols denoting the key, the time, the movement, expression, etc., so that he may hum the air from the visualized notes, with expression and with correct interpretation. Changes of key, time or movement should be carefully noted in the memorization of the notes. And above everything else, memorize the *feeling* of that particular portion of the score, that you may not only see and hear, but also *feel* that which you are recalling.

We would advise the student to practice memorizing simple songs at first, for various reasons. One of these reasons is that these songs lend themselves readily to memorizing, and the chain of easy association is usually maintained throughout.

In this phase of memory, as in all others, we add the advice to: Take interest; bestow Attention; and Practice and Exercise as often as possible. You may have tired of these words—but they constitute the main principles of the development of a retentive memory. Things must be impressed upon the memory, before they may be recalled. This should be remembered in every consideration of the subject.

Chapter 16

How to Remember Occurrences

The phase of memory which manifests in the recording of and recollection of the occurrences and details of one's every-day life is far more important than would appear at first thought. The average person is under the impression that he remembers very well the occurrences of his every-day business, professional or social life, and is apt to be surprised to have it suggested to him that he really remembers but very little of what happens to him during his waking hours. In order to prove how very little of this kind is really remembered, let each student lay down this book, at this place, and then quieting his mind let him endeavor to recall the incidents of the same day of the preceding week. He will be surprised to see how very little of what happened on that day he is really capable of recollecting. Then let him try the same experiment with the occurrences of yesterday—this result will also excite surprise. It is true that if he is reminded of some particular occurrence, he will recall it, more or less distinctly, but beyond that he will remember nothing. Let him imagine himself called upon to testify in court, regarding the happenings of the previous day, or the day of the week before, and he will realize his position.

The reason for his failure to easily remember the events referred to is to be found in the fact that he made no effort at the time to impress these happenings upon his subconscious mentality. He allowed them to pass from his attention like the proverbial "water from the duck's back." He did not wish to be bothered with the recollection of trifles, and in endeavoring to escape from them, he made the mistake of failing to store them away. There is a vast difference between dwelling on the past, and storing away past records for possible future reference. To allow the records of each day to be destroyed is like tearing up the important business papers in an office in order to avoid giving them a little space in the files.

It is not advisable to expend much mental effort in fastening each important detail of the day upon the mind, as it occurs; but there is an easier way that will accomplish the purpose, if one will but take a little trouble in that direction. We refer to the practice of *reviewing* the occurrences of each day, after the active work of the day is over. If you will give to the occurrences of each day a mental review in the evening, you will find that the act of reviewing will employ the attention to such an extent as to register the happenings in such a manner that they will be available if ever needed thereafter. It is akin to the filing of the business papers of the day, for possible future reference. Besides this advantage, these reviews will serve you well as a reminder of many little things of immediate importance which have escaped your recollection by reason of something that followed them in the field of attention.

You will find that a little practice will enable you to review the events of the day, in a very short space of time, with a surprising degree of accuracy of detail. It seems that the mind will readily respond to this demand upon it. The process appears to be akin to a mental digestion, or rather a mental rumination, similar to that of the cow when it "chews the cud" that it has previously gathered. The thing is largely a "knack" easily acquired by a little practice. It will pay you for the little trouble and time that you expend upon it. As we have said, not only do you gain the advantage of storing away these records of the day for future use, but you also have your attention called to many important details that have escaped you, and you will find that many ideas of importance will come to you in your moments of leisure "rumination." Let this work be done in the evening, when you feel at ease—but do not do it after you retire. The bed is made for sleep, not for thinking. You will find that the subconsciousness will awaken to the fact that it will be called upon later for the records of the day, and will, accordingly, "take notice" of what happens, in a far more diligent and faithful manner. The subconsciousness responds to a call made upon it in an astonishing manner, when it once understands just what is required of it. You will see that much of the virtue of the plan recommended consists in the fact that in the review there is an employment of the attention in a manner impossible during the haste and rush of the day's work. The faint impressions are brought out for examination, and the attention of the examination and review greatly deepen the impression in each case, so that it may be reproduced thereafter. In a sentence: it is *the deepening of the faint impressions of the day.*

Thurlow Weed, a well-known politician of the last century, testifies to the efficacy of the above mentioned method, in his "Memoirs." His plan was slightly different from that mentioned by us, but you will at once see that it involves the same principles—the same psychology. Mr. Weed says: "Some of my friends used to think that I was 'cut out' for a politician, but I saw at once a fatal weakness. My memory was a sieve. I could remember nothing. Dates, names, appointments, faces—everything escaped me. I said to my wife, 'Catherine, I shall never make a successful politician, for I cannot remember, and that is a prime necessity of politicians. A politician who sees a man once should remember him forever.' My wife told me that I must train my memory. So when I came home that night I sat down alone and spent fifteen minutes trying silently to recall with accuracy the principal events of the day. I could remember but little at first—now I remember that I could not then recall what I had for breakfast. After a few days' practice I found I could recall more. Events came back to me more minutely, more accurately, and more vividly than at first. After a fortnight or so of this, Catherine said 'why don't you relate to me the events of the day instead of recalling them to yourself? It would be interesting and my interest in it would be a stimulus to you.' Having great respect for my wife's opinion, I began a habit of oral confession, as it were, which was continued for almost fifty years. Every night, the last thing before retiring, I told her everything I could remember that had happened to me, or about me, during the day. I generally recalled the very dishes I had for breakfast, dinner and tea; the people I had seen, and what they had said; the editorials I had written for my paper, giving her a brief abstract of them; I mentioned all the letters I had seen and received, and the very language used, as nearly as possible; when I had walked or ridden—I told her everything that had come within my observation. I found that

I could say my lessons better and better every year, and instead of the practice growing irksome, it became a pleasure to go over again the events of the day. I am indebted to this discipline for a memory of unusual tenacity, and I recommend the practice to all who wish to store up facts, or expect to have much to do with influencing men."

The careful student, after reading these words of Thurlow Weed, will see that in them he has not only given a method of recalling the particular class of occurrences mentioned in this lesson, but has also pointed out a way whereby the entire field of memory may be trained and developed. The habit of reviewing and "telling" the things that one perceives, does and thinks during the day, naturally sharpens the powers of future observation, attention and perception. If you are witnessing a thing which you know that you will be called upon to describe to another person, you will instinctively apply your attention to it. The knowledge that you will be called upon for a description of a thing will give the zest of interest or necessity to it, which may be lacking otherwise. If you will "sense" things with the knowledge that you will be called upon to tell of them later on, you will give the interest and attention that go to make sharp, clear and deep impressions on the memory. In this case the seeing and hearing has "a meaning" to you, and a purpose. In addition to this, the work of review establishes a desirable habit of mind. If you don't care to relate the occurrences to another person—learn to tell them to yourself in the evening. Play the part yourself. There is a valuable secret of memory imbedded in this chapter—if you are wise enough to apply it.

Chapter 17

How to Remember Facts

In speaking of this phase of memory we use the word "fact" in the sense of "an ascertained item of knowledge," rather than in the sense of "a happening," etc. In this sense the Memory of Facts is the ability to store away and recollect items of knowledge bearing upon some particular thing under consideration. If we are considering the subject of "Horse," the "facts" that we wish to remember are the various items of information and knowledge regarding the horse, that we have acquired during our experience—facts that we have seen, heard or read, regarding the animal in question and to that which concerns it. We are continually acquiring items of information regarding all kinds of subjects, and yet when we wish to collect them we often find the task rather difficult, even though the original impressions were quite clear. The difficulty is largely due to the fact that the various facts are associated in our minds only by contiguity in time or place, or both, the associations of relation being lacking. In other words we have not properly classified and indexed our bits of information, and do not know where to begin to search for them. It is like the confusion of the business man who kept all of his papers in a barrel, without index, or order. He knew that "they are all *there*" but he had hard work to find any one of them when it was required. Or, we are like the compositor whose type has become "pied," and then thrown into a big box—when he attempts to set up a book page, he will find it very difficult, if not impossible—whereas, if each letter were in its proper "box," he would set up the page in a short time.

This matter of association by relation is one of the most important things in the whole subject of thought, and the degree of correct and efficient thinking depends materially upon it. It does not suffice us to merely "know" a thing—we must know where to find it when we want it. As old Judge Sharswood, of Pennsylvania, once said: "It is not so much to know the law, as to know *where to find it.*" Kay says: "Over the associations formed by contiguity in time or space we have but little control. They are in a manner accidental, depending upon the order in which the objects present themselves to the mind. On the other hand, association by similarity is largely put in our own power; for we, in a measure, select those objects that are to be associated, and bring them together in the mind. We must be careful, however, only to associate together such things as we wish to be associated together and to recall each other; and the associations we form should be based on fundamental and essential, and not upon mere superficial or casual resemblances. When things are associated by their accidental, and not by their essential qualities,—by their superficial, and not by their fundamental relations, they will not be available when wanted, and will be of little real use. When we associate what is new with what most nearly resembles it in the mind already, we give it its proper place in our fabric of thought. By means of association by similarity, we tie up our ideas, as it were, in separate bundles, and it is of the utmost importance that all the ideas that most nearly resemble each other be in one bundle."

The best way to acquire correct associations, and many of them, for a separate fact that you wish to store away so that it may be recollected when needed—some useful bit of information or interesting bit of knowledge, that "may come in handy" later on—is to *analyze* it and its relations. This may be done by asking yourself questions about it—each thing that you associate it with in your answers being just one additional "cross-index" whereby you may find it readily when you want it. As Kay says: "The principle of asking questions and obtaining answers to them, may be said to characterize all intellectual effort." This is the method by which Socrates and Plato drew out the knowledge of their pupils, filling in the gaps and attaching new facts to those already known. When you wish to so consider a fact, ask yourself the following questions about it:

I. Where did it come from or originate?

II. What caused it?

III. What history or record has it?

IV. What are its attributes, qualities and characteristics?

V. What things can I most readily associate with it? What is it like?

VI. What is it good for—how may it be used—what can I do with it?

VII. What does it prove—what can be deduced from it?

VIII. What are its natural results—what happens because of it?

IX. What is its future; and its natural or probable end or finish?

X. What do I think of it, on the whole—what are my general impressions regarding it?

XI. What do I know about it, in the way of general information?

XII. What have I heard about it, and from whom, and when?

If you will take the trouble to put any "fact" through the above rigid examination, you will not only attach it to hundreds of convenient and familiar other facts, so that you will remember it readily upon occasion, but you will also create a new subject of general information in your mind of which this particular fact will be the central thought. Similar systems of analysis have been published and sold by various teachers, at high prices—and many men have considered that the results justified the expenditure. So do not pass it by lightly.

The more other facts that you manage to associate with any one fact, the more pegs will you have to hang your facts upon—the more "loose ends" will you have whereby to pull that fact into the field of consciousness—the more cross indexes will you have whereby you may "run down" the fact when you need it. The more associations you attach to a fact, the more "meaning" does that fact have for you, and the more interest will be created regarding it in your mind. Moreover, by so doing, you make very probable the "automatic" or involuntary recollection of that fact when you are thinking of some of its associated subjects; that is, it will come into your mind naturally in connection with something else—in a "that reminds me" fashion. And the oftener that you are involuntarily "reminded" of it, the clearer and deeper does its impression become on the records of your memory. The oftener you use a fact, the easier does it become to recall it when needed. The favourite pen of a man is always at his hand in a remembered position, while the less used eraser or similar thing has to be searched for, often without success. And the more associations that you bestow upon a fact, the oftener is it likely to be used.

Another point to be remembered is that the future association of a fact depends very much upon your system of filing away facts. If you will think of this when endeavoring to store away a fact for future reference, you will be very apt to find the best mental pigeon-hole for it. File it away with *the thing it most resembles*, or to which it has the most familiar relationship. The child does this, involuntarily—it is nature's own way. For instance, the child sees a zebra, it files away that animal as "a donkey with stripes;" a giraffe as a "long-necked horse;" a camel as a "horse with long, crooked legs, long neck and humps on its back." The child always attaches its new knowledge or fact on to some familiar fact or bit of knowledge—sometimes the result is startling, but the child remembers by means of it nevertheless. The grown up children will do well to build similar connecting links of memory. Attach the new thing to some old familiar thing. It is easy when you once have the knack of it. The table of questions given a little farther back will bring to mind many connecting links. Use them.

If you need any proof of the importance of association by relation, and of the laws governing its action, you have but to recall the ordinary "train of thought" or "chain of images" in the mind, of which we become conscious when we are day-dreaming or indulging in reverie, or even in general thought regarding any subject. You will see that every mental image or idea, or recollection is associated with and connected to the preceding thought and the one following it. It is a chain that is endless, until something breaks into the subject from outside. A fact flashes into your mind, apparently from space and without any reference to anything else. In such cases you will find that it occurs either because you had previously set your subconscious mentality at work upon some problem, or bit of recollection, and the flash was the belated and delayed result; or else that the fact came into your mind because of its association with some other fact, which in turn came from a precedent one, and so on. You hear a distant railroad whistle and you think of a train; then of a journey; then of some distant place; then of someone in that place; then of some event in the life of that person; then of a similar event in the life of another person; then of that other person; then of his or her brother; then of that brother's last business venture; then of that business; then of some other business resembling it; then of some people in that other business; then of their dealings with a man you know; then of the fact that another man of a similar name to the last man owes you some money; then of your determination to get that money; then you make a memorandum to place the claim in the hands of a lawyer to see whether it cannot be collected now, although the man was "execution proof" last year—from distant locomotive whistle to the possible collection of the account. And yet, the links forgotten, the man will say that he "just happened to think of" the debtor, or that "it somehow flashed right into my mind," etc. But it was nothing but the law of association—that's all. Moreover, you will now find that whenever you hear mentioned the term "association of mental ideas," etc., you will remember the above illustration or part of it. We have forged a new link in the chain of association for you, and years from now it will appear in your thoughts.

Chapter 18

How to Remember Words, Etc.

In a preceding chapter we gave a number of instances of persons who had highly developed their memory of words, sentences, etc. History is full of instances of this kind. The moderns fall far behind the ancients in this respect; probably because there does not exist the present necessity for the feats of memory which were once accepted as commonplace and not out of the ordinary. Among ancient people, when printing was unknown and manuscripts scarce and valuable, it was the common custom of the people to learn "by heart" the various sacred teachings of their respective religions. The sacred books of the Hindus were transmitted in this way, and it was a common thing among the Hebrews to be able to recite the books of Moses and the Prophets entirely from memory. Even to this day the faithful Mohammedans are taught to commit the entire Koran to memory. And investigation reveals, always, that there has been used the identical process of committing these sacred books to memory, and recalling them at will—the natural method, instead of an artificial one. And therefore we shall devote this chapter solely to this method whereby poems or prose may be committed to memory and recalled readily.

This natural method of memorizing words, sentences, or verses is no royal road. It is a system which must be mastered by steady work and faithful review. One must start at the beginning and work his way up. But the result of such work will astonish anyone not familiar with it. It is the very same method that the Hindus, Hebrews, Mohammedans, Norsemen, and the rest of the races, memorized their thousands of verses and hundreds of chapters of the sacred books of their people. It is the method of the successful actor, and the popular elocutionist, not to mention those speakers who carefully commit to memory their "impromptu" addresses and "extemporaneous" speeches.

This natural system of memorizing is based upon the principle which has already been alluded to in this book, and by which every child learns its alphabet and its multiplication table, as well as the little "piece" that it recites for the entertainment of its fond parents and the bored friends of the family. That principle consists of the learning of one line at a time, and reviewing that line; then learning a second line and reviewing that; and then reviewing the two lines together; and so on, each addition being reviewed in connection with those that went before. The child learns the sound of "A;" then it learns "B;" then it associates the sounds of "A, B" in its first review; the "C" is added and the review runs: "A, B, C." And so on until "Z" is reached and the child is able to review the entire list from "A to Z," inclusive. The multiplication table begins with its "twice 1 is 2," then "twice 2 is 4," and so on, a little at a time until the "twos" are finished and the "threes" begun. This process is kept up, by constant addition and constant review, until "12 twelves" finishes up the list, and the child is able to repeat the "tables" from first to last from memory.

But there is more to it, in the case of the child, than merely learning to repeat the alphabet or the multiplication table—there is also the strengthening of the memory as a result of its exercise and use. Memory, like every faculty of the mind, or every muscle of the body, improves and develops by intelligent and reasonable use and exercise. Not only does this exercise and use develop the memory along the particular line of the faculty used, but also along *every* line and faculty. This is so because the exercise develops the power of concentration, and the use of the voluntary attention.

We suggest that the student who wishes to acquire a good memory for words, sentences, etc., begin at once, selecting some favourite poem for the purpose of the demonstration. Then let him memorize one verse of not over four to six lines to begin with. Let him learn this verse perfectly, line by line, until he is able to repeat it without a mistake. Let him be sure to be "letter perfect" in that verse—so perfect that he will "see" even the capital letters and the punctuation marks when he recites it. Then let him stop for the day. The next day let him repeat the verse learned the day before, and then let him memorize a second verse in the same way, and just as perfectly. Then let him review the first and second verses together. This addition of the second verse to the first serves to weld the two together by association, and each review of them together serves to add a little bit to the weld, until they become joined in the mind as are "A, B, C." The third day let him learn a third verse, in the same way and then review the three. Continue this for say a month, adding a new verse each day and adding it to the verses preceding it. But constantly review them from beginning to end. He cannot review them too often. He will be able to have them flow along like the letters of the alphabet, from "A" to "Z" if he reviews properly and often enough.

Then, if he can spare the time, let him begin the second month by learning *two verses* each day, and adding to those that precede them, with constant and faithful reviews. He will find that he can memorize two verses, in the second month, as easily as he did the one verse in the first month. His memory has been trained to this extent. And so, he may proceed from month to month, adding an extra verse to his daily task, until he is unable to spare the time for all the work, or until he feels satisfied with what he has accomplished. Let him use moderation and not try to become a phenomenon. Let him avoid overstraining. After he has memorized the entire poem, let him start with a new one, but not forget to revive the old one at frequent intervals. If he finds it impossible to add the necessary number of new verses, by reason of other occupation, etc., let him not fail to keep up his review work. The exercise and review is more important than the mere addition of so many new verses.

Let him vary the verses, or poems with prose selections. He will find the verses of the Bible very well adapted for such exercise, as they lend themselves easily to registration in the memory. Shakespeare may be used to advantage in this work. The "Rubaiyat" of Omar Khayyam; or the "Lady of the Lake" by Scott; or the "Song Celestial" or "Light of Asia" both by Edwin Arnold, will be found to be well adapted to this system of memorizing, the verses of each being apt to "stick in the memory," and each poem being sufficiently long to satisfy the requirements of even the most ambitious student. To look at the complete poem (any of those mentioned) it would seem almost impossible that one would ever be able to memorize and recite it from beginning to end, letter perfect. But on the principle of the continual dripping of water wearing away the stone; or the snowball increasing at each roll; this practice of a little being associated to what he already has will soon allow him to accumulate a wonderfully large store of memorized verses, poems, recitations, etc. It is an actual demonstration of the catchy words of the popular song which informs one that: "Every little bit, added to what you've got, makes just a little bit more."

After he has acquired quite a large assortment of memorized selections, he will find it impossible to review them all at one time. But he should be sure to review them all at intervals, no matter how many days may elapse between each review.

The student who has familiarized himself with the principles upon which memory depends, as given in the preceding chapters, will at once see that the three principles of attention, association and repetition are employed in the natural method herein recommended. Attention must be given in order to memorize each verse in the first place; association is employed in the relationship created between the old verses and the new ones; and repetition is employed by the frequent reviewing, which serves to deepen the memory impression each time the poem is repeated. Moreover, the principle of interest is invoked, in the gradual progress made, and the accomplishment of what at first seemed to be an impossible task—the game element is thus supplied, which serves as an incentive. These combined principles render this method an ideal one, and it is not to be wondered that the race has so recognized it from the earliest times.

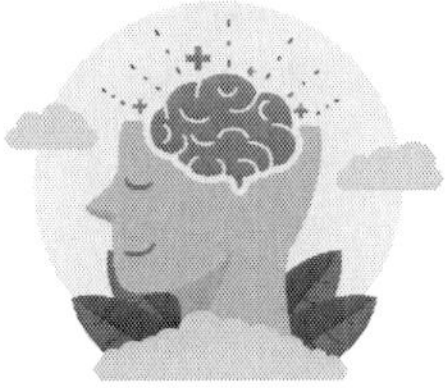

Chapter 19

How to Remember Books, Plays, Tales, Etc.

In the preceding chapters we have given you suggestions for the development of the principal forms of memory. But there are still other phases or forms of memory, which while coming under the general classification may be still considered as worthy of special consideration. For instance there may be suggestions given regarding the memorization of the contents of the books you read, the stories you hear, etc. And so we have thought it advisable to devote one chapter to a consideration of these various phases of memory that have been "left out" of the other chapters.

Many of us fail to remember the important things in the books we read, and are often mortified by our ignorance regarding the contents of the works of leading authors, or of popular novels, which although we have read, we have failed to impress upon the records of our memory. Of course we must begin by reminding you of the ever present necessity of interest and attention—we cannot escape from these principles of the memory. The trouble with the majority of people is that they read books "to kill time," as a sort of mental narcotic or anæsthetic, instead of for the purpose of obtaining something of interest from them. By this course we not only lose all that may be of importance or value in the book, but also acquire the habit of careless reading and inattention. The prevalence of the habit of reading many newspapers and trashy novels is responsible for the apparent inability of many persons to intelligently absorb and remember the contents of a book "worthwhile" when they do happen to take up such a one. But, still, even the most careless reader may improve himself and cure the habit of inattention and careless reading.

Noah Porter says: "We have not *read* an author till we have seen his object, whatever it may be, as he *saw* it." Also: "Read with attention. This is the rule that takes precedence of all others. It stands instead of a score of minor directions. Indeed it comprehends them all, and is the golden rule... The page should be read as if it were never to be seen a second time; the mental eye should be fixed as if there were no other object to think of; the memory should grasp the facts like a vise; the impressions should be distinctly and sharply received." It is not necessary, nor is it advisable to attempt to *memorize* the text of a book, excepting, perhaps, a few passages that may seem worthy to be treasured up word for word. The principal thing to be remembered about a book is its *meaning*—what it is about. Then may follow the general outline, and the details of the story, essay, treatise or whatever it may be. The question that should be asked oneself, after the book is completed, or after the completion of some particular part of the book, is: "What was the writer's idea—what did he wish to say?"

Get the *idea* of the writer. By taking this mental attitude you practically place yourself in the place of the writer, and thus *take part* in the idea of the book. You thus view it from the inside, rather than from the outside. You place yourself at the centre of the thing, instead of upon its circumference.

If the book be a history, biography, autobiography, narrative, or story of fact or fiction, you will find it of value to visualize its occurrences as the story unfolds. That is, endeavor to form at least a faint mental picture of the events related, so that you see them "in your mind's eye," or imagination. Use your imagination in connection with the mechanical reading. In this way you build up a series of mental pictures, which will be impressed upon your mind, and which will be remembered just as are the scenes of a play that you have witnessed, or an actual event that you have seen, only less distinct of course. Particularly should you endeavor to form a clear mental picture of each character, until each one is endowed with at least a semblance of reality to you. By doing this you will impart a naturalness to the events of the story and you will obtain a new pleasure from your reading. Of course, this plan will make you read more slowly, and many trashy tales will cease to interest you, for they do not contain the real elements of interest—but this is no loss, but is a decided gain for you. At the end of each reading, take the time to mentally review the progress of the story—let the characters and scenes pass before your mental vision as in a moving picture. And when the book is finally completed, review it as a whole. By following this course, you will not only acquire the habit of easily remembering the tales and books that you have read, but will also obtain much pleasure by re-reading favourite stories in your imagination, years after. You will find that your favourite characters will take on a new reality for you, and will become as old friends in whose company you may enjoy yourself at any time, and whom you may dismiss when they tire you, without offense.

In the case of scientific treatises, essays, etc., you may follow a similar plan by dividing the work into small sections and mentally reviewing the *thought*—(not the words) of each section until you make it your own; and then by adding new sections to your review, you may gradually absorb and master the entire work. All this requires time, work and patience, but you will be repaid for your expenditure. You will find that this plan will soon render you impatient at books of little consequence, and will drive you to the best books on any given subject. You will begin to begrudge your time and attention, and hesitate about bestowing them upon any but the very best books. But in this you gain.

In order to fully acquaint yourself with a book, before reading it you should familiarize yourself with its general character. To do this you should pay attention to the full title, and the sub-title, if there be any; the name of the author and the list of other books that he has written, if they are noted on the title page, or the one preceding it, according to the usual custom. You should read the preface and study carefully the table of contents, that you may know the field or general subject covered by the book—in other words endeavor to get the general outline of the book, into which you may afterwards fill in the details.

In reading a book of serious import, you should make it a point to fully grasp the meaning of each paragraph before passing on to the next one. Let nothing pass you that you do not understand, at least in a general way. Consult the dictionary for words not familiar to you, so that you may grasp the full idea intended to be expressed. At the end of each chapter, section and part, you should review that which you have read, until you are able to form a mental picture of the general ideas contained therein.

To those who wish to remember the dramatic productions that they have attended, we would say that the principles above mentioned may be applied to this form of memory as well as to the memory of books. By taking an interest in each character as it appears; by studying carefully each action and scene, and then reviewing each act in the intervals between the acts; and by finally reviewing the entire play after your return home; you will fasten the whole play as a complete mental picture, on the records of your memory. If you have acquainted yourself with what we have just said regarding the recollection of the contents of books, you will be able to modify and adapt them to the purpose of recollecting plays and dramatic productions. You will find that the oftener you review a play, the more clearly will you remember it. Many little details overlooked at first will come into the field of consciousness and fit into their proper places.

Sermons, lectures and other discourses may be remembered by bestowing interest and attention upon them, and by attempting to grasp each general idea advanced, and by noting the passage from one general idea to another. If you will practice this a few times, you will find that when you come to review the discourse (and this you should always do—it is the natural way of developing memory) the little details will come up and fit into their proper places. In this form of memory, the important thing is to train the memory by exercise and review. You will find that at each review of a discourse you will have made progress. By practice and exercise, the subconscious mentality will do better work, and will show that it is rising to its new responsibilities. You have allowed it to sleep during the many discourses to which you have listened, and it must be taught new habits. Let it know that it is expected to retain that which it hears, and then exercise it frequently by reviews of discourses, and you will be surprised at the degree of the work it will perform for you. Not only will you remember better, but you will *hear* better and more intelligently. The subconsciousness, knowing that it will be called upon later on to recollect what is being said, will urge you to bestow the attention necessary to supply it with the proper material.

To those who have had trouble in remembering discourses, we urge that they should begin to attend lectures and other forms of discourse, with the distinct purpose of developing that form of memory. Give to the subconscious mentality the positive command that it shall attend to what is being said, and shall record the same in such a way that when you review the discourse afterward you will be presented with a good synopsis or syllabus of it. You should avoid any attempt to memorize the *words* of the discourse—your purpose being to absorb and record the *ideas* and general thought expressed. Interest—Attention—Practice—Review—these are the important points in memory.

To remember stories, anecdotes, fables, etc., the principles given above are to be employed. The main thing in memorizing an anecdote is to be able to catch the *fundamental idea* underlying it, and the epigrammatic sentence, or central phrase which forms the "point" of the story. Be sure that you catch these perfectly, and then commit the "point" to memory. If necessary make a memorandum of the point, until you have opportunity to review the story in your mind. Then carefully review it mentally, letting the mental image of the idea pass before you in review, and then repeating it to yourself in your own words. By rehearsing and reviewing the story, you make it your own and will be able to relate it afterward just as you would something that you had actually experienced. So true is this principle, that when carried too far it endows the story with a false sense of actuality—who has not known men who told a story so often that they came actually to believe it themselves? Do not carry the principle to this extreme but use it in moderation. The trouble with many men is that they attempt to repeat a tale, long after they have heard it, without reviewing or rehearsing in the meantime. Consequently they omit many important points, because they have failed to impress the story as a whole upon the memory. In order to *know* an anecdote properly, one should be able to *see* its characters and incidents, just as he does when he sees an illustrated joke in a comic paper. If you can make a mental picture of an anecdote, you will be apt to remember it with ease. The noted story tellers review and rehearse their jokes, and have been known to try them on their unsuspecting friends in order to get the benefit of practice before relating them in public—this practice has been called by flippant people: "trying it on the dog." But it has its good points, and advantages. It at least saves one the mortification of being compelled to finish up a long-drawn out tale by an: "Er—well, um-m-m—I'm afraid I've forgotten just how that story ended—but it was a good one!"

Chapter 20

General Instructions

In this chapter we shall call your attention to certain of the general principles already mentioned in the preceding chapters, for the purpose of further impressing them upon your mind, and in order that you may be able to think of and to consider them independent of the details of the special phases of memory. This chapter may be considered in the nature of a general review of certain fundamental principles mentioned in the body of the work.

Point I. *Give to the thing that you wish to memorize, as great a degree of concentrated attention as possible.*

We have explained the reason for this advice in many places in the book. The degree of concentrated attention bestowed upon the object under consideration, determines the strength, clearness and depth of the impression received and stored away in the subconsciousness. The character of these stored away impressions determines the degree of ease in remembrance and recollection.

Point II. *In considering an object to be memorized, endeavor to obtain the impressions through as many faculties and senses as possible.*

The reason for this advice should be apparent to you, if you have carefully read the preceding chapters. An impression received through both sound and sight is doubly as strong as one received through but one of these channels. You may remember a name, or word, either by having seen it in writing or print; or else by reason of having heard it; but if you have both *seen and heard* it you have a double impression, and possess two possible ways of reviving the impression. You are able to remember an orange by reason of having seen it, smelt it, felt it and tasted it, and having heard its name pronounced. Endeavor to know a thing from as many sense impressions as possible—use the eye to assist ear-impressions; and the ear to assist in eye-impressions. See the thing from as many angles as possible.

Point III. *Sense impressions may be strengthened by exercising the particular faculty through which the weak impressions are received.*

You will find that either your eye memory is better than your ear memory, or vice versa. The remedy lies in exercising the weaker faculty, so as to bring it up to the standard of the stronger. The chapters of eye and ear training will help you along these lines. The same rule applies to the several phases of memory—develop the weak ones, and the strong ones will take care of themselves. The only way to develop a sense or faculty is to intelligently train, exercise and use it. Use, exercise and practice will work miracles in this direction.

Point IV. *Make your first impression strong and firm enough to serve as a basis for subsequent ones.*

Get into the habit of fixing a clear, strong impression of a thing to be considered, from the first. Otherwise you are trying to build up a large structure upon a poor foundation. Each time you revive an impression you deepen it, but if you have only a dim impression to begin with, the deepened impressions will not include details omitted in the first one. It is like taking a good sharp negative of a picture that you intend to enlarge afterward. The details lacking in the small picture will not appear in the enlargement; but those that *do* appear in the small one, will be enlarged with the picture.

Point V. *Revive your impressions frequently and thus deepen them.*

You will know more of a picture by seeing it a few minutes every day for a week, than you would by spending several hours before it at one time. So it is with the memory. By recalling an impression a number of times, you fix it indelibly in your mind in such a way that it may be readily found when needed. Such impressions are like favourite tools which you need every little while—they are not apt to be mislaid as are those which are but seldom used. Use your imagination in "going over" a thing that you wish to remember. If you are studying a thing, you will find that this "going over" in your imagination will help you materially in disclosing the things that you have not remembered about it. By thus recognizing your weak points of memory, you may be able to pick up the missing details when you study the object itself the next time.

Point VI. *Use your memory and place confidence in it.*

One of the important things in the cultivation of the memory is the actual use of it. Begin to trust it a little, and then more, and then still more, and it will rise to the occasion. The man who has to tie a string around his finger in order to remember certain things, soon begins to cease to use his memory, and in the end forgets to remember the string, or what it is for. There are many details, of course, with which it is folly to charge the memory, but one should never allow his memory to fall into disuse. If you are in an occupation in which the work is done by mechanical helps, then you should exercise the memory by learning verses, or other things, in order to keep it in active practice. Do not allow your memory to atrophy.

Point VII. *Establish as many associations for an impression, as possible.*

If you have studied the preceding chapters, you will recognize the value of this point. Association is memory's method of indexing and cross-indexing. Each association renders it easier to remember or recollect the thing. Each association gives you another string to your mental bow. Endeavor to associate a new bit of knowledge with something already known by, and familiar to you. In this way to avoid the danger of having the thing isolated and alone in your mind—without a label, or index number and name, connect your object or thought to be remembered with other objects or thoughts, by the association of contiguity in space and time, and by relationship of kind, resemblance or oppositeness. Sometimes the latter is very useful, as in the case of the man who said that "Smith reminds me so much of Brown—he's so *different*." You will often be able to remember a thing by remembering something else that happened at the same place, or about the same time—these things give you the "loose ends" of recollection whereby you may unwind the ball of memory. In the same way, one is often able to recollect names by slowly running over the alphabet, with a pencil, until the sight of the capital first letter of the name brings the memory of those following it—this, however, only when the name has previously been memorized by *sight*. In the same way the first few notes of a musical selection will enable you to remember the whole air; or the first words of a sentence, the entire speech or selection following it. In trying to remember a thing which has escaped you, you will find it helpful to think of something associated with that thing, even remotely. A little practice will enable you to recollect the thing along the lines of the faintest association or clue. Some men are adept memory detectives, following this plan. The "loose end" in memory is all the expert requires. Any associations furnish these loose ends. An interesting and important fact to remember in this connection is that if you have some one thing that tends to escape your memory, you may counteract the trouble by noting the associated things that have previously served to bring it into mind with you. The associated thing once noted, may thereafter be used as a loose end with which to unwind the elusive fact or impression. This idea of association is quite fascinating when you begin to employ it in your memory exercises and work. And you will find many little methods of using it. But always use natural association, and avoid the temptation of endeavoring to tie your memory up with the red-tape of the artificial systems.

Point VIII. *Group your impressions.*

This is but a form of association, but is very important. If you can arrange your bits of knowledge and fact into logical groups, you will always be master of your subject. By associating your knowledge with other knowledge along the same general lines, both by resemblances and by opposites, you will be able to find what you need just when you need it. Napoleon Bonaparte had a mind trained along these lines. He said that his memory was like a large case of small drawers and pigeon-holes, in which he filed his information according to its kind. In order to do this he used the methods mentioned in this book of comparing the new thing with the old ones, and then deciding into which group it naturally fitted. This is largely a matter of practice and knack, but it may be acquired by a little thought and care, aided by practice. And it will repay one well for the trouble in acquiring it. The following table will be found useful in classifying objects, ideas, facts, etc., so as to correlate and associate them with other facts of a like kind. The table is to be used in the line of questions addressed to oneself regarding the thing under consideration. It somewhat resembles the table of questions given in Chapter XVII, of this book, but has the advantage of brevity. Memorize this table and use it. You will be delighted at the results, after you have caught the knack of applying it.

Query Table. *Ask yourself the following questions regarding the thing under consideration. It will draw out many bits of information and associated knowledge in your mind:*

(1) WHAT?

(2) WHENCE?

(3) WHERE?

(4) WHEN?
(5) HOW?
(6) WHY?
(7) WHITHER?

While the above Seven Queries are given you as a means of acquiring clear impressions and associations, they will also serve as a Magic Key to Knowledge, if you use them intelligently. If you can answer these questions regarding anything, you will know a great deal about that particular thing. And after you have answered them fully, there will be but little unexpressed knowledge regarding that thing left in your memory. Try them on some one thing—you cannot understand them otherwise, unless you have a very good imagination.

OTHER HARDBACK BOOKS

- 1984 by George Orwell
  Fiction/Classics, ISBN: 9788193545836
- Abraham Lincoln by Lord Charnwood
  Biographies/Leaders, ISBN: 9789387669147
- Alice's Adventures in Wonderland by Lewis Carroll
  Children's/Classics, ISBN: 9789387669055
- Animal Farm by George Orwell
  Fiction/Classics, ISBN: 9789387669062
- Anthem by Ayn Rand
  Fiction/Classics, ISBN: 9789389157178
- As a Man Thinketh by James Allen
  Fiction/Classics, ISBN: 9789388118422
- Awakened Imagination by Neville Goddard
  Religion & Spirituality, ISBN: 9789389157185
- Be What You Wish by Neville Goddard
  Mind, Body & Spirit, ISBN: 9789388118163
- Becoming a Writer by Dorothea Brande
  Self Help/General, ISBN: 9789389157192
- Believe in Yourself by Joseph Murphy
  Mind, Body & Spirit, ISBN: 9789388118439
- Black Beauty by Anna Sewell
  Children's/Classics, ISBN: 9789388118262
- Civilization and Its Discontents by Sigmund Freud
  Social Sciences/General, ISBN: 9789388118279
- Demian by Hermann Hesse
  Fiction/Classics, ISBN: 9789388118170
- Feeling is the Secret by Neville Goddard
  Religion & Spirituality, ISBN: 9789389157208

Search the book by its ISBN

OTHER HARDBACK BOOKS

- Gitanjali by Rabindranath Tagore
  Fiction/Poems, ISBN: 9789387669079
- Great Speeches of Abraham Lincoln by Abraham Lincoln
  History/United States, ISBN: 9789387669154
- How to Attract Money by Joseph Murphy
  Self Help/Success, ISBN: 9789388118446
- How to be Filled with the Holy Spirit by A.W. Tozer
  Religion/Christianity, ISBN: 9789389157215
- How to Enjoy Your Life and Your Job by Dale Carnegie
  Self Help/General, ISBN: 9789388118293
- Illust. Biography of William Shakespeare by Manju Gupta
  Biographies/Authors, ISBN: 9789387669246
- Madhubala by Manju Gupta
  Biographies/Cinems, ISBN: 9789387669253
- Mansarover 1 (Hindi) by Premchand
  Fiction/Short Stories, ISBN: 9789387669086
- Meditations by Marcus Aurelius
  Non Fiction/Philosopy, ISBN: 9789388118781
- My Inventions: The Autobio. of Nikola Tesla by Nikola Tesla
  Autobiographies/Scientists, ISBN: 9789388118187
- Selected Stories of Rabindranath Tagore by Rabindranath Tagore
  Fiction/Short Stories, ISBN: 9789387669307
- Sense and Sensibility by Jane Austen
  Fiction/Classics, ISBN: 9789387669109
- Siddhartha by Hermann Hesse
  Fiction/Classics, ISBN: 9789387669116
- Tales from India by Rudyard Kipling
  Fiction/Short Stories, ISBN: 9789387669123

Search the book by its ISBN

OTHER HARDBACK BOOKS

- The Tales from Shakespeare by Charles Lamb, Mary Lamb
  Fiction/Short Stories, ISBN: 9789387669314
- The Alchemy of Happiness by Al-Ghazzali
  Religion & Spirituality, ISBN: 9789388118309
- The Art of Public Speaking by Dale Carnegie
  Self Help/General, ISBN: 9789388118477
- The Autobiography of a Yogi by Paramahansa Yogananda
  Autobiographies/General, ISBN: 9789387669192
- The Dynamic Laws of Prosperity by Catherine Ponder
  Mind, Body & Spirit, ISBN: 9789388118194
- The Elements of Style by William Strunk
  Non Fiction/Skill, ISBN: 9789389157222
- The Game of Life and How to Play It by Florence Scovel Shinn
  Mind, Body & Spirit, ISBN: 9789388118316
- The Imitation of Christ by Thomas À Kempis
  Religion/Christianity, ISBN: 9789388118200
- The Jungle Book by Rudyard Kipling
  Children's/Classics, ISBN: 9789387669338
- The Knowledge of the Holy by A.W. Tozer
  Religion/Christianity, ISBN: 9789389157239
- The Light of Asia by Sir Edwin Arnold
  Fiction/Poetry, ISBN: 9789387669130
- The Magic of Faith by Joseph Murphy
  Mind, Body & Spirit, ISBN: 9789388118712
- The Origin of Species by Charles Darwin
  Sciences/Life Sciences, ISBN: 9789387669345
- The Path of Prosperity by James Allen
  Mind, Body & Spirit, ISBN: 9789388118323

Search the book by its ISBN

OTHER HARDBACK BOOKS

- The Power of Awareness by Neville Goddard
  Mind, Body & Spirit, ISBN: 9789388118330
- The Power of Concentration by Theron Q. Dumont
  Self Help/General, ISBN: 9789388118224
- The Power of Positive Thinking by Norman Vincent Peale
  Mind, Body & Spirit, ISBN: 9789388118729
- The Prophet by Kahlil Gibran
  Fiction/Classics, ISBN: 9789388118453
- The Psychopathology of Everyday Life by Sigmund Freud
  Non Fiction/Psychology, ISBN: 9789388118231
- The Pursuit of God by A.W. Tozer
  Religion/Christianity, ISBN: 9789389157246
- The Quick and Easy Way to Effec. Speaking by Dale Carnegie
  Self Help/General, ISBN: 9789388118347
- The Science of Getting Rich by Wallace D. Wattles
  Self Help/Success, ISBN: 9789387669239
- The Seven Laws of Teaching by John Milton Gregory
  Self Help/General, ISBN: 9789388118460
- The Upanishads by Swami Paramananda
  Religion/Hinduism, ISBN: 9789388118774
- The World as I See It by Albert Einstein
  Non Fiction/Philosopy, ISBN: 9789388118248
- Thought Vibration by William Walker Atkinson
  Non Fiction/Philosopy, ISBN: 9789389157253
- Wake Up and Live! by Dorothea Brande
  Mind, Body & Spirit, ISBN: 9789388118255
- Your Faith is Your Fortune by Neville Goddard
  Religion & Spirituality, ISBN: 9789389157260

Search the book by its ISBN